Showdown at Stony Crest

Also by Joseph Wayne
in Large Print:

The Gun and the Law

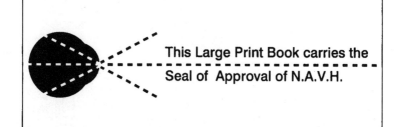

This Large Print Book carries the
Seal of Approval of N.A.V.H.

Showdown at Stony Crest

Published in 2002 by arrangement with Golden West
Literary Agency.

Thorndike Press Large Print Western Series.

The tree indicium is a trademark of Thorndike Press.

The text of this Large Print edition is unabridged.
Other aspects of the book may vary from the original edition.

Cover design by Thorndike Press Staff.

Set in 16 pt. Plantin by Elena Picard.

Printed in the United States on permanent paper.

Library of Congress Cataloging-in-Publication Data

Wayne, Joseph, 1906–
    Showdown at Stony Crest / by Joseph Wayne.
        p. cm.
    ISBN 0-7862-4249-3 (lg. print : hc : alk. paper)
    1. Large type books. 2. Revenge — Fiction. 3. Colorado
— Fiction. I. Title.
PS3529.V33 S56 2002
    813′.54—dc21   2002020256

Showdown at Stony Crest

Joseph Wayne

Thorndike Press • Waterville, Maine

Chapter One

Cole Knapp rode through the dark-timbered passages of the La Sal Mountains and down into Paradox Valley with its high, bare walls, buff and red and white, bright-hued from the misty rain that was driven against them by a wind that was cool for June. Sagebrush, damp and dripping, gave off an odor both pungent and pleasant. A rock, loosened by rain, thundered off the rim to raise a low rumble on the valley floor.

A big man, this Cole Knapp, but thin with riding and slim trail rations. Hide and bone and muscle, and travel-stained from the countless miles which lay between southern Arizona where he had started, and the western slope of Colorado where he now was.

The gun at his right thigh was almost a part of him; a part of him, too, was the vengeful burning he had brought with him all the way from Arizona.

He made no noon stop. This was new country, but he had heard enough about it to have the strange sensation that he had seen it before. A trail here, a naked ridge over there. The slick rock top of the rim where wisps of clouds trailed like banners in the air.

Overhead the black clouds were driven eastward by the wind, and thunder was a continuous, sullen promise. And then the promise was kept and the rain came down in sheets that swept across the walls of the canyon.

Cole tipped his head forward and water rolled off his Stetson and down the front of his slicker. In this moment the world became soaking wet, the road hock-deep in slippery mud and every little wash filled to overflowing with swift water as thick and brown as chocolate. The rain swept past, and ahead became a silver curtain pulled across the valley and hiding all that lay beyond.

The rain slackened by the time he reached the Dolores River and the town of Bedrock. He squinted at it with cold discomfort. Not much of a town, but he hadn't expected much. A schoolhouse, a store, a blacksmith shop and a saloon. Over the saloon door was a weathered, bullet-pocked sign, half-obliterated but still readable, *Cowboy's Rest.*

Two horses were tied at the hitch pole, heads down, rumps to the wind and rain. On their dripping hides was the Chain brand, and when Cole saw this he reined in, stepped down, and tied.

The rain had almost stopped. Westward across the Dolores the edge of the sky was a blue slot between horizon and clouds. Behind Cole thunder tapered off to a low rumble up among the high peaks of the La Sals.

Cole stepped onto the porch of the saloon. Mud that had been deep dust a few hours before now balled on his boots. Swearing mildly, he scraped his feet on the ends of the worn boards and went inside.

"Clean your feet, mister," the bartender said irritably. "I've been pushing mud through that door all afternoon."

"They're clean enough." Cole unbuttoned his slicker as he crossed to the bar. He took off his hat and batted it against his knee to remove the water which still clung to it. "When it rains around here it rains."

"And all runs off," the bartender agreed sourly.

The two Chain men studied Cole with curious neutrality. One was tall with a thin, pock-marked face. The other was short and dark. Run-of-the-mill cowhands, Cole thought. He might have found them in an Arizona bar or a New Mexico cantina as easily as here in Colorado close to the Utah line.

"What'll it be?" the bartender asked, swiping idly with a damp cloth in front of Cole.

"Whisky," Cole said.

He rang a coin on the bar as a bottle and glasses were placed before him. Then he dropped his purposeful bombshell: "I'm a stranger hereabouts. I'm looking for a man named Andy Carew. Know where I can find him?"

From a corner of his eye he saw the two cowboys' faces tighten with quick interest, saw their hastily exchanged glances, and the curtain of caution drop down across their eyes.

The bartender motioned toward them. "They work for the Carews. Maybe they can tell you, but me, I never heard of an Andy Carew."

"We didn't either," the tall cowboy said. He hitched at his pants and turned from the bar, trying to appear casual. "See you some other time, Mick."

"Wait a minute," Cole said. "If you're working for the Carews, it's damned funny you never heard of Andy."

Both men were edging toward the door. The short one muttered without looking at Cole, "We've only been on the payroll since April. If there ever was an Andy Carew, he was gone a long time before that."

The tall one added, "Only one Carew left now, mister. A girl. It's her that owns Chain. Old Bill Carew cashed in his chips last month." He turned to his partner. "We'd better ride or Marty'll be wantin' to know what we do to earn our thirty and beans."

They left quickly, obviously relieved to be getting out of the saloon. Cole turned back to the bartender. "They've heard of Andy Carew, all right. Any fool could tell that."

The bartender was silent, his eyes telling Cole nothing. "Who's this Marty they mentioned?" Cole asked.

The bartender shrugged. "Marty Keldson. He's ramrod of Chain. I think he's some kind of shirttail relation to the Carew tribe."

"How did old man Carew die? Sudden?"

"A stroke. He was getting on." The bartender moved away and picked up the glasses the Chain hands had left. As Cole swung around toward the door, the bartender called, "Don't you want your drink?"

"You drink it," Cole said. "I got what I came for."

He paused on the porch, watching the Chain men riding away. They rode fast, their horses' hoofs throwing up huge gobs of mud behind. They hit the bridge spanning the Dolores and hoofs thudded against the sodden planks. At the far side they looked back.

Cole smiled wryly as he mounted. By sundown or sooner, Marty Keldson would know there was a stranger in the country, and that the stranger was asking for Andy Carew.

Cole crossed the bridge after forcing his horse to take the unfamiliar footing. The Dolores was high and roily, heavy with silt and mud. Feathery tamarisk on the west bank drooped under the weight of the rain.

Now, in early June, the snow would be melting fast in the high country. Probably this was the peak of the run-off.

In late afternoon Cole left the valley, swinging to the south across a broken country of mesas covered by cedars and piñon pines. The trail threaded up through the gaps in the rimrock and across a boulder-strewn arroyo, then on to the next steep slope. The clouds were breaking up now, and in the distance he could see the peaks of the San Juan Range, their saw-teeth combing the sky.

Rain had not reached this far, but the wind running down from the La Sals behind him carried the clean, sharp smell of it. There was the aroma of pine and sagebrush, and the scent of sun-warmed cedars and piñons all around him. The smell of dust, too, for here it had apparently not rained for weeks.

The grass grew in bunches instead of a mat of sod. A good stock country, Cole thought. And it seemed to stretch away forever. He passed no ranches, not even a nester's shack; but there were steers on these mesas, fine and fat and sleek of hide. Four-year-olds, he judged, that would weigh close to thirteen hundred pounds after the summer on this grass.

Chain range reached from the Dolores behind him to Lord knew where to north and south. Its vastness spoke well for Bill Carew. Or did it? Cole knew there was always the other side, the side of little men with dreams and hopes, men who had settled here and been moved on by Chain guns.

Near sunset he rode down off the last mesa. A long valley opened before him, a valley with a brawling stream running through it between walls of willow shoots. At the base of the mesa, the stream swung north toward the San Miguel, which, Cole knew, was a tributary of the Dolores. Ahead of Cole was a town.

From the height of the mesa, he had made out the cluster of houses, the cottonwoods, the columns of smoke rising into the evening air. Supper time, with children demanding at the tops of their shrill voices when it would be time to eat, and men walking slowly home from work. A small and peaceful town called Cedar that for years had lived under the shadow of Chain.

Somewhere in town was a lawyer, Judge Fred Benson. Perhaps he was one of those now going home from work. But Cole would see him in the morning. Not tonight. No sense to hurry. He was playing a poker hand that he had to bet before he could know his most formidable opponent or see any of their cards. Tomorrow would be time enough.

He made camp between the stream and a deserted stone cabin that stood fifty feet from the willows. He stripped gear from his horse and staked him out in the tall valley grass.

Then he built a fire, boiled the last of his coffee, and cooked the last of a piece of venison he had killed a week ago. Eating, he thought with pleasure of the breakfast he'd

14

have tomorrow in town — half a dozen eggs, and ham, and all the coffee he could drink. Maybe he'd even eat a wedge of pie for breakfast.

He rinsed out his blackened coffeepot in the stream, and scrubbed his skillet with sand. Then he stepped into the cabin out of pure curiosity and began to kick around in the debris.

Not much left, just the stone walls and the roof. A splintered table leaned crazily against one wall. The legs of a chair. The cracked head of a doll, its body chewed away by rats.

He went outside and built up his fire against the night that he knew would be cold at this altitude. He brought armloads of dead wood from among the willows and piled them near the fire. Then he squatted beside it, idly comfortable, and stared into the flames reflectively.

He knew the kind of man Bill Carew must have been to build a ranch like Chain. And he could guess what had happened here, what probably had happened a dozen other places up and down the creek and out on the mesas wherever there was water.

To these places families had brought their dreams. But the Chain crew would come, led by this giant of a man, this Bill Carew, and their guns would be close to their hands. Maybe there would be a few shots if the nester was stubborn. But always the ultimatum: "Keep moving. You can't settle here. This is Chain range and it always will be."

And so they had left. Miles down the trail a little girl had remembered her doll and wept. But a frightened father would not turn back. There were other lands, and other dolls, but there was no other life once the spark had gone.

Darkness moved in and the stars came out, burning glittering holes in the empty blackness of the limitless sky. Far away Cole could still hear the low rumble of thunder up among the lofty peaks of the La Sals, and occasionally heat lightning flickered and danced upon the horizon.

A coyote yipped, high on the near-by rim, and another answered. Soon the night was filled with their racket and that of the dogs in town, answering this kindred call. Presently this died out and there was only the thunder.

Cole lost track of time. He was tired, but oddly enough, not sleepy. He thought of the doll head he had found, and of Bill Carew, now dead. He wondered what Chain was like with the great man gone.

What was the Carew girl like? And the foreman, Marty Keldson? Could a ranch that had grown fat over the clean-picked bones of little men change? Or would it always be the devouring force Bill Carew had made it until it was worn to nothing by the erosion of time?

He let his mind go back over the weeks to the little Arizona town of San Ramon, to Andy Carew who had been the best friend Cole Knapp ever had, and who lay dying with a dry gulcher's bullet in his back. He would never forget those last whispered words, "See about my sister Sidonie, Cole. If she needs any help, give it to her." He would, of course, but something else had brought him back. He had trailed Andy's killer to this range; and now he would find out who it was — and kill him.

Suddenly Cole was aware of the steady beat of horses coming toward him across the grass. Instinctively he rose and moved away from the fire toward the stone wall of the cabin. He had learned long ago that a man didn't stay by the fire in a strange country. Especially a man who had come to kill, or be killed.

The horses were closer now, coming hard from the east. Cole listened, his head tipped for a minute, or maybe two. Then a rider burst into the pool of light and Cole, surprised, saw that it was a girl.

"I saw your fire," the girl said. "Who is it?"

Cole stepped away from the wall. "What's the matter?"

"Who are you?"

The riders were closer now. "Get down. Hide in the willows. Quick."

She obeyed, not questioning him. He slipped the bridle from the mare and slapped her rump with it. The mare ran off into the darkness. Cole threw the bridle onto his own pile of gear, and stepped back to the wall.

Now the pursuing riders were upon him, pulling up just outside the fringe of firelight, one of them demanding in a rough voice, "You see anybody, mister? Or hear a horse?"

Cole's hand touched the grip of his gun. He knew that they could see him no more clearly than he saw them. "I heard a horse," he said.

"Which way was he going?"

"West, friend. Where else could he go, with you coming at him from the east?"

They went on at once, hoofs drumming solidly against the ground until at last all sound was lost. But they'd be back. The mare wouldn't run very hard without a rider. Even if they didn't find the mare, they'd return when they reached the end of the valley, and they'd question him.

He saw the girl moving out of the willow thicket, still a shadowy figure in the darkness. He called softly, "Stay there. They'll be back."

"Who are you?" she asked.

"My name's Cole Knapp. What's yours?" He liked her voice, now that most of the panic was out of it.

"Sidonie Carew," she answered.

He could still see her, a vaguely lighted shape at the edge of the willows, and he searched his mind for some explanation to fit this strange situation. Here was the Carew girl who owned Chain. But why, of all the people in the valley, was she being chased?

He heard the horses again, still traveling hard, coming back. He said quickly, "Go deeper into the willows and stay perfectly still. No matter what happens, don't come out. You understand?"

She did not answer, but he heard her moving back.

Again he stepped toward the cabin so he would have the stone wall at his back. And he waited, while the approaching hoofbeats grew from a distant rumble to a ground-shaking thunder.

Chapter Two

This time the three riders swept into the firelight before they reined in. From the milling
group of horses, the same rough voice came at
Cole. "What'd you do with her?"

The tone rubbed against Cole's temper
like sandpaper. "Her? You need a pack to
chase girls in this country?"

"Where is she? We know she's here, and
we know it's the Carew girl. We found her
mare down the valley a piece."

"Let it go, Dick," a man on the far side
said. "We know what we aimed to know."

"Not yet, Pomeroy," the man called Dick
said. "I want to talk to her. Where is she?"

"Talk to me if you've got to talk," Cole
said.

Dick rode close and looked down at Cole.
"Friend, you're new around here, so I'll tell
you something you'd better know. I'm Dick
Walters, president of the Regulators. I want
to talk to the girl. Just talk. Now for the last

time, where's she at?"

"All right, so you're a big man on this range, but you're wasting your time. There's no girl here to talk to."

"I figure there is. And I figure she's in that cabin. I'm going to have a look."

Walters moved as though to dismount. Cole's thumb slipped from his cartridge belt and his hand fell naturally to the grips of his gun. He said, "Stay on your horse. Stay on your horse, and I'll tell you something you'd better know. I came here to settle with a man. Maybe it's you and maybe it ain't. But don't push. Don't ever try to push me."

The man on the far side spoke again, this time with quick alarm. "All right, all right. Dick ain't pushin' you. And we don't make a habit of chasin' girls. But she was spyin' on our meetin' tonight. We figured it was a Chain cowhand and we were fixin' to teach him a lesson."

"Now you know it wasn't. So drag it, boys."

Walters called out, "Don't let me see you around here again! We know how to handle your kind." Then he whirled his horse and set his spurs. The three disappeared into the night, riding as hard as they had ridden before.

This was Cole's first night here, but already the pattern of hate and fear was plain — a familiar pattern that a man could find on any range, in any town; only here it was stronger, more virulent.

Bill Carew had sown the seeds, probably a long time ago. Now that he was dead, someone had to reap the harvest. Maybe the someone would be this girl out there in the willows.

Cole waited until the sound of retreating hoofs died to the east, then he called, "You can come out now. I don't think they'll be back."

He stooped and threw several sticks of wood on the fire. When he straightened, she was standing before him in the firelight. "Thank you, Mr. Knapp," she said, her voice calm. "I doubt if they'd have hurt me, but I didn't want to talk to them and I'm glad I didn't have to."

Cole said nothing. Standing on the other side of the fire from her, he had his first good chance to observe Sidonie Carew. She was about twenty, he judged, slender and straight-backed and proud. But her pride was not the haughty arrogance he might have expected to find in Bill Carew's daughter. Instead, it was a quiet thing of dignity and self-assurance, exactly like her brother Andy.

She was not really beautiful. Her mouth was too long, her cheekbones a trifle high, but she was attractive, her face alive. She was the kind of girl, he thought, who enjoyed every minute she was awake.

Her eyes were either gray or blue. He couldn't quite be sure in the poor light from the fire. Suddenly she dropped her gaze from his appraising stare, and now he noticed the way she was dressed. She wore a flat-topped Stetson held in place by a chin strap, a leather jacket over a tan blouse, and a dark green, split riding skirt. Her face was deeply tanned — not the tan of a few days in the sun, but rather the smooth bronze of one who has spent many hours outside.

She glanced up at him, smiling. "I suppose you're wondering about some things."

Cole nodded.

"The Regulators Walters mentioned are a bunch of greasy sack ranchers who live above the town of Cedar," she said. "A hardcase named Bud Davis was their leader until he was killed a few months ago. Now Walters has taken his place. They're jealous of Chain because it's big. They're lazy, too. They live off our beef and they'll steal our grass if they can. But Chain belongs to me and I don't intend to let them steal our range."

She looked at her boot and toed the edge of the fire. "My father died last month." She lifted her head and he saw something like defiance in her eyes. "Dad was the best cowman for two hundred miles around. He wouldn't have left me the biggest spread on the western slope if he hadn't been. Now he's gone; so men like Walters want to start chipping away at Chain."

"They said you'd been spying on them."

"I was. I was in town when I heard about their meeting, so I didn't have time to go home after one of my men. I tried to listen at Walters's window, but I stumbled and made a noise. They came after me and I ran. I saw your fire; so I took a chance that whoever was here would get them off my neck."

Cole rolled a cigarette. Bending over the fire, he lighted it with a flaming twig. He wondered if her story were as simple as it sounded. Were the Regulators chipping away at Chain, or was the shoe on the other foot? Maybe she did own Chain, but did she run it? It was an important question as far as Cole was concerned, but not one he could ask now.

He straightened, and tossed the twig back into the fire. He thought her face was flushed, but she said steadily enough, "I'm wondering something about you, too."

"What's that?"

"You said you came here to settle with a man."

Cole laughed easily. "Talk. Just big talk." He had earlier considered telling her about Andy and about Andy's death. Now he decided against it after hearing her condemn the Regulators. She'd probably take everything he told her straight to Keldson.

"I'm not so sure it is big talk."

"I'll saddle up and see if I can find your mare," Cole said. "Then I'll take you home."

"You don't need to do that."

"No, I don't need to, but I'm going to."

He turned from her, picked up his bridle and walked to his horse. He saddled the animal and rode down the creek, leaving the girl at the fire staring after him.

Why didn't she want him to take her home? Would seeing Chain, its crew and foreman, prove her previous claim against the small ranchers to be untrue? He suspected it would. Usually the smaller outfits were glad enough to be let alone. It was the big ones who pushed, and Bill Carew had owned a big spread.

He wondered if the girl had deliberately lied to him, and admitted the possibility that she simply didn't know the situation.

The paint mare was skittish when he found her, and without a bridle he had to run her a hundred yards before he could catch up and drop his loop over her head. But once the rope tightened, she became docile and quiet. He led her back to the fire, dismounted, and put on the girl's bridle. Sidonie stepped into the saddle at once, saying, "I'm not far from home. You don't —"

"I'm taking you home."

"I owe you something, but that doesn't mean you can —"

"Are you afraid of me, Miss Carew?"

For a moment she stared at him, her jaw set firmly. Finally she said stiffly, "I guess I can't stop you if you insist on riding with me."

"That's right," he said.

She rode out of the circle of firelight, and Cole swung to the saddle and fell in beside her.

For a time they followed the creek, winding through the willows and deadfalls along a path apparently familiar to Sidonie. Then they left it, and crossed a grassy expanse of meadow, afterward climbing through low, cedar-covered hills. At last they struck a road which wound upward in a series of switchbacks to the top of the mesa.

The valley stretched below them, and in its center Cole saw a tight little group of lights — the town of Cedar. This fitted the pattern which was beginning to form in Cole's mind.

A man like Bill Carew would look down upon other men. He would build his ranch so he could always look down, holding in contempt the timid ones who depended upon each other for protection as well as for company.

The buildings of Chain were directly ahead of them. Cole asked, "Was this the original location of the ranch?"

She didn't answer at once, and he felt her hostility in the hesitation. At last she said, "No, the old place was about five miles from here."

"Then these buildings are new?"

"They're eight years old."

"Why did your father move here?"

"He never told me. Why are you so interested, Mr. Knapp?"

"I've got an inquiring mind."

The ranch house was a dark and sprawling shape before them, its only lights in the front part of the house. In the starlight he could make out dimly the other buildings. There would be the usual barns, sheds, corrals, bunkhouse, and cook shack. Somewhere there would be a chicken house and perhaps a place for a few turkeys.

They reined in before the house. As Cole stepped down, Sidonie said, "You were going to bring me home, Mr. Knapp. You have."

Cole looped his reins around the hitch pole. He said, "I was raised kind of proper, ma'am. I'll see you to your door."

She swung down and stood close to him, looking up. "You helped me and I told you I was grateful," she said. "What else am I supposed to do?"

"Take me into the house. Maybe your mother will offer me a cup of coffee."

"My mother died when I was small."

"I'm sorry." He paused, then added, "Somebody's in the house. There's sure to be coffee on the stove. Maybe Marty Keldson —"

"Who are you?" Fear was suddenly in her voice.

"Knapp. Cole Knapp. I told you that."

"I know you did. I also heard you tell Dick Walters you came here to kill a man, or as you put it, to settle with him. Who?"

"I don't know."

"But Marty Keldson might do for a start. Is that it?"

"You just stop worrying, Miss Carew," he said, making his voice gentle. "All I want is a cup of coffee."

She stood not more than a step from him, her head tipped back so she could look into his face. He heard her quick breathing, as though she had been running. Finally she said, "I own Chain, but according to my father's will the management of it falls upon my stepmother until I'm twenty-one. Marty is her son by a previous marriage. He's the one who really runs Chain. He's unpredictable and dangerous, Mr. Knapp. Don't come in. Don't cross him."

"Afraid for me? Or for yourself?"

"Not for myself."

"Then I'll go in. I'd like to meet Marty Keldson."

"All right," she said wearily. "I've warned you. Now you deserve whatever happens to you."

She whirled and walked stiff-backed along the path toward the house. He caught up and in silence followed her to the door.

Chapter Three

Sidonie opened the front door and stood aside for Cole to enter. He found himself in a long hall, dimly lighted by a lamp in a wall bracket, its far end lost in darkness. She shut the door behind him, saying crisply, "This way, Mr. Knapp."

She opened a door on the left, and again stood aside for him to go past her into the room beyond. She closed the door. "I'll call my stepmother," she said, and walked away, her boot heels making staccato clicks against the hardwood floor.

Cole stopped two steps away from the hall door, hat in hand, staring at what he supposed was the living-room of the ranch house. He didn't know what he had expected, but certainly not this.

Here was grandeur such as might have been expected in mining camps where paupers became rich overnight, where ostentatious display was the rule and a measure of the success a man had attained. Yet why such a display here, on this lonely ranch, forty miles from the nearest railroad? What had Bill Carew needed to prove?

Everything, the expensive plush-upholstered furniture, the oak wall paneling, the Oriental carpets, shouted of money lavishly spent. And the room had a fragrance, a smell of leather and fine fabrics, and a hint of perfume.

A door opened quietly at the far end of the enormous room. Cole heard a rustle of silk, and was suddenly conscious of his own appearance. He hadn't shaved for a week. His clothes were caked with dust and sweat, and smelled of campfire smoke and horse, of the sagebrush of the plains and the pine of the mountains.

He grinned ruefully, rubbing his stubbled face. He'd practically forced his way in here and it served him right. Now he had to stay.

He remained where he was until the two women reached him. Sidonie smiled as though enjoying his discomfort. She said, "Zelda, I want to present Mr. Cole Knapp. Mr. Knapp, this is my stepmother, Mrs. William Carew."

Formality was out of place in the range country, but somehow it fitted this room. Yet the spark in Sidonie's eyes told Cole she

31

was baiting him, repaying him for his stubborn insistence.

He found Mrs. Carew as surprising as the room in which he stood. About forty-five, she was a tall, handsome woman who carried herself in a regal manner that fitted her surroundings. Even before she spoke, he sensed that she was a woman of great pride and vanity.

Her features were regular, almost to the point of perfection. Her eyes were brown and her hair, coiled atop her head as though she sought this added height, was so black it held bluish, metallic glints. It had no hint of gray.

Her dress was black silk, its skirt reaching to the floor. A white lace collar fitted snugly and sedately around her neck. A gold watch was pinned over her left breast, its cover holding an intricate floral design through which were cleverly worked the initials, *Z.C.* A ruby set in the center of the cover glittered in the lamplight like an overbright red star.

For a moment Mrs. Carew's dark eyes appraised him, then she smiled and offered her hand. "Welcome to Chain, Mr. Knapp. Sidonie tells me you went out of your way to help her, so let me add my thanks to hers."

Cole took her hand, finding it soft-skinned, and released it quickly. "No need for thanks," he said. "I'd have done —"

Sidonie broke in. "Mr. Knapp, Zelda would love to show you around. She planned this house herself, you know."

Zelda looked pleased. "Thank you, my dear." She drew a breath. "As you can see, Mr. Knapp, it's a terribly expensive —" She looked at him, plainly trying not to notice the condition of his clothes. She began again. "My husband, Mr. Carew, died last month as you no doubt know. The end came after a lingering illness, and I miss him terribly."

"I'm sorry."

She touched her eyes with a lace handkerchief. "He was a wonderful and generous man. He did his best to gratify every foolish whim I had."

Cole didn't speak. There was no need for it. Zelda, once started, would take care of the talking. He glanced quickly at Sidonie, detecting a real malice in her eyes.

He turned his gaze back to Zelda who was walking toward the foot of the stairs which led to the floor above. "Perhaps you didn't notice when you came in, Mr. Knapp, because of the darkness. But the house is built of stone. One of our greatest difficulties was transportation. Everything, including the stone, had to come by narrow-gauge to

33

Placerville and then be hauled here by wagons."

She pointed to the stairs. "The staircase is made of Italian marble. I have seen such marble in State buildings, but seldom in a private home."

She turned from the stairway and gestured toward the door through which Cole and Sidonie had entered. "The dining-room is across the hall. I won't take time to show it to you, but you'll be interested in knowing that the walls are of satin tapestry, and the trim is of red mahogany. A rare combination, Mr. Knapp."

She faced Cole, making a sweeping, inclusive gesture. "This is our reception room. When we built the house, Mr. Carew considered going into politics and expected to do a great deal of entertaining. Unfortunately, he was so busy with his cattle business that he just never got started in politics."

Cole smiled, suspecting that the political ambitions had been Zelda's.

She went on, "The floor is of walnut, and the walls of solid oak paneling. It goes clear to the ceiling which, as you can see, is white with oak trim in Gothic design. We had most of the furniture especially made of oak to fit the decor of the room. But for my hus-

band's sake, we had a few pieces uphol-
stered with red plush. Mr. Carew was a man
who liked his comfort."

She started across the room again, mo-
tioning graciously for him to follow. "These
French doors open into the conservatory.
I'd like you to notice the vine-trellised windows and the potted palms —"

Cole interrupted. "Mrs. Carew, I want to
ask a question —"

She was so absorbed that she apparently
didn't hear. She paused again, this time before the stone fireplace, and pointed to the
huge portrait above it in a gaudy gilt frame.
"Before we go into the conservatory, I'd like
to show you this portrait of my husband. He
was a great man, Mr. Knapp, a great pio-
neer. He brought his first herd of cattle into
this country while it was still reservation
land, and the wild Indians — Utes, I believe
— were all around." She smiled at Sidonie.
"You remember some of the stories he used
to tell."

Cole stared at the giant canvas. It might
have been a portrait of an amiable,
bewhiskered pirate, which was probably exactly what Bill Carew had been. But Cole
had become impatient. He said, "Mrs.
Carew, I came here to ask you about Andy."

She turned abruptly to face him, and in

that one second ceased to be the great lady and became a human being, anxious and worried. The affectation of speech and manner magically dropped away from her.

"Andy? Why do you ask about Andy?"

"I want to see him."

"He's not here." She turned to Sidonie. "It's late, dear, I'm sure Mr. Knapp will not be here much longer."

"I am a little tired," Sidonie said. "If you'll excuse me, I'll go upstairs to my room."

Halfway to the top of the stairs, she paused to look back over her shoulder, the hint of a mocking smile lingering on her lips. "Good night, Mr. Knapp. Or perhaps I should say good-by. Men like you are always on the move, so I'm sure I won't see you again."

Cole grinned back at her. "You'll see me. I'm done with moving on — for now at least."

It pleased him to see her smile fade into a long, level stare. He saw concern in her face, and perhaps something close to fear. The last he saw of her were her feet and trim ankles below the hem of her riding skirt.

He turned back to Zelda. She asked, "Who are you, Mr. Knapp?" her gaze as direct as her question.

"Cole Knapp. The name's not an alias, if

that's what you mean."

"But who are you? Where did you come from? Why are you here asking for Andy?"

Cole hadn't heard the opening of the hall door. He wasn't sure he heard a sound at all. But suddenly he felt another presence in the room. He glanced around. A man stood in the hall doorway, a big man in range garb who was as completely out of place in this room as Cole was.

"What's the trouble?" the man asked.

"No trouble," Zelda Carew said quickly. "This is my son, Marty Keldson, Mr. Knapp. Now that Mr. Carew is dead, Marty is in charge of Chain."

Keldson didn't speak. He tipped his head a bare half inch in acknowledgment of Cole's presence and that was all. Cole nodded back, returning Keldson's stare and feeling the skin tighten on the back of his neck.

Marty Keldson was nearly six feet tall; but being heavy of bone and muscle, and broad of shoulder, he gave the impression of being shorter than he actually was. His face was wide, almost square. Something about him, perhaps his cool silence, perhaps the way his muscled shoulders threatened to break through his worn blue shirt gave Cole the impression of contemptuous arrogance.

37

Mrs. Carew's voice broke the silence. "I asked you some questions, Mr. Knapp."

He brought his gaze away from Keldson with an effort.

"I asked a question, too, and I didn't get an answer," he said.

Her voice became fretful. "I can't tell you much about Andy. He was Sidonie's brother and my husband's only son." She put a hand on the mantel as though to steady herself. He had a feeling she was frightened, however hard she tried to conceal it.

He glanced at Keldson, wondering how a refined, graceful woman such as Zelda Carew could have borne a son like Keldson. He was human dross, while Zelda seemed to be pure, fine gold.

"I haven't seen Andy for nine years," she said. "He quarreled with his father and left home. We never had a letter from him. He simply disappeared. Do you know where he is?"

"Would I be here asking for him if I knew?"

"I don't know. I don't know at all." Her fine airs were gone now; she was a distressed and frightened woman.

Cole turned toward the hall door, and discovered that Marty Keldson was gone. He reached for the knob.

"This is a troubled range, Mr. Knapp," Zelda said. "The men who call themselves the Regulators are nothing but outlaws who are trying to destroy us. You saw what happened tonight to Sidonie. I don't know what you intend to do, but whatever it is, you will only add to the trouble we already have and make trouble for yourself. You had better leave the country."

He looked back at her, and his eyes lifted involuntarily to the portrait of Bill Carew. Another freak of heredity, he thought. It seemed as unlikely that Carew could have sired Sidonie as it did that Zelda could have borne Keldson.

He said, "I'm sorry, Mrs. Carew, but I've got to stay. There must be somebody somewhere who can tell me about Andy."

He went out, closing the door firmly behind him. An odd smile lingered on his mouth all the way to his horse. The trap was set. Sooner or later someone would take the bait.

Looking back at the house, he wondered what had possessed Bill Carew to build it. He must have loved his wife very deeply to have satisfied her extravagant whims. Or else he'd been mad with power and arrogance.

He untied his horse and for a moment

stood motionless, troubled by a vague sense that something was wrong. A voice called to him from the shadows, "Hold it, Knapp. Hold it right where you are."

The voice was Marty Keldson's, as heavy and arrogant as the man himself.

"I've got a shotgun," Keldson said. "You've been around some, friend. You know what a shotgun can do against a six-shooter at this range."

"I know." Cole held himself motionless.

"Then listen, because I never warn a man twice. Get out of this country. Andy Carew don't mean a damned thing to anybody around here. He quarreled with his old man nine years ago and rode out of the country. When Bill died, we tried to trace him, but we never picked up a smell. So he's gone. Maybe dead. Now you get out of the country and leave him stay dead, or you'll be damned sorry. You savvy?"

"I'm still listening."

"Maybe I'd better make it plainer. I'm going to marry Sidonie. She owns this outfit and I intend to see that her rights are protected. No damned ridge runner like you is going to come around clouding her title with a stink about Andy. If he'd wanted his share of Chain, he could have stuck around, and if you're trying to cut yourself in, you're gonna get a pine overcoat and a six-by-three piece of real estate. Now get to hell out of here."

"Finished?"

"Yeah. Get on your horse and ride. And keep riding."

There was violence in Keldson's voice, and Cole remembered what Sidonie had said about him being unpredictable.

He mounted and let his horse walk into the darkness. He understood now why Sidonie was afraid of Keldson. Surely she didn't intend to marry him. Cole couldn't think, at the moment, of anything worse that could happen to her.

Andy had been gone a long time; he had only known Marty as a boy, but he had guessed the kind of man he would be. Again Cole let his thoughts go back to the way it had been between him and Andy.

Cole had been town marshal in San Ramon, Andy a stage driver. Andy was gone much of the time, but they'd been together a good deal, too, enough to talk about many things, but never about the home Andy had left. Cole had been curious, but it wasn't a thing he could ask about. Andy would tell him when he wanted to and no sooner.

In April a stranger showed up in San Ramon and asked for Andy. At first Cole thought the man was a bounty hunter and that Andy was wanted by the law, but it turned out that Judge Benson here in Cedar was trying to locate him. The stranger claimed to be a detective and he said Andy's dad was sick, but Andy was to stay in San Ramon until he was sent for.

After that Andy had told Cole how it had been at home. After Andy's mother died, Bill Carew married Zelda and when she came to Chain she brought Marty with her. Andy hadn't got along with Marty from the first, and he hadn't liked Zelda. Marty was sly, starting fights with Andy for no good reason, and when Zelda had finished working on the old man, he always blamed Andy for starting the trouble. Finally Andy couldn't stand it any longer, had a row with the old man and left home.

After Cole heard that, he tried to get Andy to go home, but Andy was stubborn. He said his dad would send for him directly if he wanted him, so Cole had to let it stand. One night early in May Andy was shot in the back when he was on his way home after he'd brought the stage in from Tucson. He lived only a few minutes after Cole reached him.

Cole read the sign by lantern light, but there wasn't much to learn. A stranger had been staying in the San Ramon hotel, and he disappeared after the shooting. Cole followed him, losing the trail and picking it up again until it led to Andy's home range.

It must, Cole thought, have been Marty Keldson who had been behind Andy's murder. Keldson had the most to gain from Andy's death. He had no proof, but he'd find it. He'd stay here until he did.

Chapter Four

Cole camped for the night along the creek below the mesa, and rode into the town of Cedar early. He had watched the sun come up over the San Juans and poke its searching rays into the lower end of the valley after first sliding them off the mesa he had descended the day before. Mountains and hills before him had been shrouded by purple shadows that had shrunk steadily until now they clung only in the deep gorges close under the rims.

Good summer range up there high, Cole thought. Chain range, he could be sure of that. Bill Carew had built his empire in the days when the country belonged to the Utes, according to Zelda Carew. And Bill Carew had wound up with everything, hay meadows along the streams, winter range on these mesas and in the cedar-and-piñon-covered hills nearby. His summer range would be up there in the high country, among aspens and spruce.

44

He must have made a fortune from it or he'd never have been able to build the mansion on the north mesa. Looking up, Cole could see the house from the valley, a rambling stone structure as out of place as a knife fight in a drawing-room.

Had it been designed entirely to Zelda Carew's whims? Or had it satisfied something within Bill Carew himself? Cole didn't know, but he did know about Chain with Marty Keldson ramrodding it. He wouldn't be satisfied with what Carew had gained. He was a man who would have to prove himself to Sidonie and the country, and to himself. Yes, Keldson was a driver. He'd be adding to Chain, and he'd never surrender an inch.

The upper valley ranchers, those who called themselves the Regulators, and perhaps the townsmen as well, were facing a more uncertain future than they'd faced while Bill Carew was alive. They probably knew it, too. Cole doubted that they actually were the outlaws both Sidonie and Mrs. Carew had said they were.

The day promised to be a hot one. The sky was blue and clear; the only clouds Cole saw nested far to the east among the granite peaks. Dust made a deep covering on the street, and a sudden gust of wind, breathing down the trough of the valley, raised a dun cloud that made Cole tip his head and tug his Stetson down. Then it was gone, but the smell of dust remained in the air.

The rain of yesterday had not reached this far east. Judging from the wilting weeds along the edge of the street and the depth of the dust, there had been no rain in Cedar for weeks. Yet even without it, the hay meadows on both sides of town and up the valley were a rich, dark green. As long as the ranchers along the creek could flood their meadows, they could hang on in spite of anything Keldson could do. Here, as in all the semi-arid West, a flowing stream was the life blood of the country.

Under the probing rays of the morning sun, the town of Cedar was revealed as a straggling, unplanned community. Even the bold façade of false fronts failed to add a note of dignity, for almost all the houses and business establishments needed paint. Weeds had grown tall in vacant lots, and all kinds of litter clung to the fences and along the edges of the boardwalks, even tumble-weeds uprooted by the winds of winter and fall.

Cole passed a church, its steeple peeling under the erosion of sun and rain. A house, surrounded by a picket fence and directly across the street, was apparently the parsonage; a sign in the front yard read, *Samuel Britton, Minister.*

Beside the parsonage was a millinery store, just beyond a drugstore, and across from these a saddle shop and the Mercantile. When Cole reached the main intersection in the center of town, he saw a sign in the shape of an arrow, pointing north. Upon it was the single word, *Chain.*

Maybe Bill Carew hadn't owned the town, but he'd used it to advertise his location just the same; even now that he was dead, his power lingered because apparently no one dared to take the sign down.

The creek paralleled Main Street. Just south of the intersection of the two roads a bridge spanned the stream. A few houses had been built on that side of the creek. Beyond, to the south, the road became a twisting tan ribbon that ran across the valley floor then climbed the mesa in a series of dizzy switchbacks.

Cole reined in at the intersection and idly shaped a smoke. Across the street he saw the Staghorn Saloon, boasting the most pretentious false front in town. At this corner also were the two-storied brick bank, the hotel, and a livery stable. East of the intersection were a few more buildings.

An elusive something distinguished this

town from the dozens of other isolated cow towns Cole had seen. He searched his mind for it; but finding it only added to his puzzlement. The town seemed completely lacking in pride and dignity.

Except for the willows along the creek there was not, as far as Cole could see, a single shade tree anywhere in town. The street was deserted except for a black and white dog dozing in the morning sun, and a rooster with a pale, droopy comb that was wallowing in the dust and making courting noises to a hen as disreputable looking as himself.

Once you sell your soul, Cole thought, you seldom find the right coin to redeem it. This was the feeling he had about Cedar. He could sense the weight of sheer inertia. This town didn't give a damn.

Cole reined into the open doors of the livery barn, and stepped down, grateful for shade and coolness after the burning rays of the sun. Cedar had surrendered long ago to Bill Carew. Now that Marty Keldson was in the driver's seat, it would have to surrender some more.

A man stepped out of a tackroom and office and came toward Cole. He wore a tarnished star on his vest, which was limp and shiny with grease and dirt. In Cole's eyes he personified the town. He was slack-lipped and walked with his shoulders bent, moving slowly as though nothing in his life was worth hurrying for.

The stableman nodded, his curious eyes moving from rider to horse and back to rider. He said, "Looks like you've come a ways."

Cole nodded. "A far piece. Give the horse a double bait of oats and rub him down."

The man stepped forward and took the reins. Cole held out his hand. "My name's Knapp. Cole Knapp."

"I'm Rhodes. Dusty Rhodes." The man's laugh was a high cackle. "Ever hear of a man named Rhodes who didn't carry the handle Dusty? Why couldn't they call some of us Muddy Rhodes? Or Icy Rhodes?"

Cole shrugged. "You the sheriff?"

"Nope. This ain't the county seat." He motioned eastward. "County seat's yonder. Mining camp, long ways from here. I'm town marshal and deputy sheriff. Not that the town needs one. Nothing ever happens in Cedar, Mr. Knapp."

It would, Cole thought, and soon. He asked, "How's the hotel?"

"Fine," Rhodes said. "For bed bugs. Sleep here if you want to." Rhodes motioned upward toward the hay-mow. "Restaurant down the street a ways. The Top Notch. Good place to eat."

Cole shook his head. "I'm staying longer than overnight. Is there someone in town who takes in boarders?"

"Can't think of nobody." Rhodes's eyes brightened. "There's Mrs. Davis, Janet Davis. They owned a ranch about five miles up the creek, but her husband got killed six, seven months ago, so she moved to town. She's havin' a hard time of it. Got no relatives but her father-in-law. That's Ben Davis. He skids cedars off'n the hills and saws 'em up for firewood. Got a steam-powered saw, he has, but don't make much with it." Rhodes swiped at a fly that settled on his nose. "She could use the money, but I doubt she'd take you. Expectin'. She's the only one, though. We don't get no strangers here."

"Where does she live?"

Rhodes shrugged. "Won't hurt to ask, I reckon." His tone said he thought it was a waste of time, but he gave the directions. "Cross the bridge and turn right. First house you come to. Can't miss it."

Cole untied his war sack from behind the saddle. Rhodes led the horse down the long, dim runway, calling back, "I'll look after him."

50

Cole walked toward the street, his war sack balanced easily on one of his powerful shoulders. He paused in the archway, but did not back up. A band of riders was coming in from the north at a dead run. Marty Keldson led them, astride a powerful blue roan. A small man on a buckskin horse rode beside Keldson. Cole counted ten men in the party and guessed it was the whole Chain crew coming in for a morning on the town.

They hauled up in a cloud of dust across the street at the Staghorn's hitch rail, and for a moment were busy tying their horses. The dog, kicked by Keldson's blue roan, yipped and streaked for the livery barn, darting between Cole's legs in his haste and confusion. The rooster and hen ran squawking toward the open space between the stable and blacksmith shop next door.

The little man who had ridden with Keldson let out a whoop, drew his gun, and fired at the elkhorns above the saloon door. Cole heard Keldson's heavy voice, "Put it up, damn it."

The men crowded past the two and into the saloon, but the little man wasn't satisfied. He called, "Hey, Dusty. Got a room with bath for a Chain man?"

Cole noticed that, with the exception of

Keldson, the little man was the only one of Chain's riders who carried a gun. Cole considered that. On some men a gun looked as out of place as two left legs. On others it seemed as much a part of them as their hands. So it was with this one. The gun was holstered low on his right thigh and tied with a thong to his leg. The holster was cut away so that the whole trigger guard was exposed.

A man like this had to be on Chain's payroll. It followed the pattern that was so familiar to Cole. Bill Carew would have needed one like him. Even if he never drew his gun against another man, he'd earn his pay just by being there.

Cole knew his type. He might have come from Abilene, or Deadwood, or Tucson. Maybe from Texas. Not a notch on his gun, but he didn't need one. The way he walked, the way he wore his gun, the steadiness in his eyes: these were enough. Men always knew him for what he was no matter where he walked or how he dressed.

Keldson recognized Cole, and even at this distance, Cole could see him stiffen with anger. Deliberately Cole left the livery stable and walked across the bridge. Behind him he heard Keldson talking to the gunslinger in words which were not distinguishable but which were plainly angry.

Cole paused on the bridge and stared back. Keldson met his stare, then turned to the small man and the pair went into the saloon.

Below Cole the water was high and roily, and along the banks tugged insistently at the willows.

Cole wondered why a man like Dusty Rhodes had accepted the star of office, why he let himself be made the butt of Chain jokes. Then he shrugged. It wasn't important. Dusty had probably been afraid to say no even more than he feared to say yes.

Cole followed a side road that turned right from the bridge. The Davis house lay just beyond, its back yard reaching to the creek. Cole noted that the house was freshly painted, the only one he'd seen in town that was.

He expected, therefore, that Mrs. Davis would be equally neat and he was not disappointed. She opened the door and nodded when Cole asked if she was Mrs. Davis.

He hesitated, realizing that he should not have come. She stood clutching the door casing, awkward and heavy with the weight of her child. Cole murmured apologetically, "I was looking for a place to stay. Rhodes in the livery stable said you might be willing —" He stopped, not quite knowing how to say what he had in mind, and more embarrassed than he cared to admit.

Mrs. Davis was a plain woman in her early twenties, but now she smiled at his discomfort and her face, bright with humor and friendliness, was suddenly not plain at all. "I understand what you're trying to say, Mr. —"

"Knapp. Cole Knapp."

"I'd like to rent you a room, Mr. Knapp. It's clean and the bed is comfortable. I'll give you your meals, too, if you want them."

Still Cole hesitated, thinking the extra burden of work was unfair. The smile left her face and was replaced by anxiety that was almost pitiful. "Won't you just look at the room before you leave? Don't let my condition worry you. I'm very well, and quite strong. I'll look after you and mend and wash your clothes —"

"I'll look at it," Cole said, and followed her into the house.

The room she showed him opened into the parlor, and was clean as she had promised. Cole dropped his war sack in a corner. When he turned to her, he found her watching him with an intensity that was almost painful. She said, "I need the money, Mr. Knapp. Every little bit helps."

"I'll stay," he said, "but if the time comes when you can't —"

"I'll tell you when it does, Mr. Knapp," she broke in. "It's a promise." She went on, chattering breathlessly as though by doing so she could regain her composure. "My father-in-law lives with me. He isn't here right now, but he'll be home this evening. He has a wood saw —"

Cole smiled and handed her a gold eagle. "When that's used up, I'll pay more. It's just that I don't know how long I'll be in town."

"Thank you. And Mr. Knapp?"

"Yes?"

"I'll have dinner for you at twelve."

Cole smiled again, liking her and oddly worried about her. He wondered how her husband had died. One of life's rotten deals, he thought as he left the house, for a woman to be widowed at her age, and with a baby that would never know its father.

He crossed the bridge again and angled across the intersection to the Staghorn. There had once been a grandeur to the saloon, he thought, but now the grandeur was tarnished and beginning to decay. A few panes of the stained glass windows, depicting an Indian in full battle dress, had been replaced by clear window glass which was dirty and fly-specked. The magnificent pair of elk antlers over the swinging doors hung askew, and some of their points had been broken off by bullets, probably fired at them by marksmen like Keldson's gunman shadow.

Cole stopped on the walk and took time to make a cigarette. He stuck it between his lips, cupped a match to its end, and then went inside.

As he walked to the bar, he saw Marty Keldson standing beside the skinny gunman near the center of the bar. The rest of Chain's crew was scattered about the big room, most of them playing poker in the rear. Dick Walters, head of the Regulators, stood at the far end of the bar, staring moodily into his beer glass. Cole recognized the man beside him as one of the three who had chased Sidonie Carew the night before.

The bartender moved toward Cole, swiping the mahogany surface with a towel. Cole said, "Beer." The bartender drew it, raked off the head with a stick, and slid it half the length of the bar. It stopped precisely in front of Cole, and Cole slid a nickel back along the same route to the white-aproned barkeep. He was sure Keldson and Walters had seen him come in, but for the present both chose to ignore him.

So Cole deliberately opened the game,

saying to the bartender in a clear voice that would carry to Walters, "It's funny about this country. I've been asking for Andy Carew ever since I showed up here, but I can't find out anything about him. He grew up here, so it looks like somebody's hiding something. Or maybe everyone wants to forget there ever was an Andy Carew."

Without looking down the bar, Cole sensed that Keldson had stiffened, that Walters and his companion were moving back from the bar and edging toward the door. Keldson walked slowly toward Cole, and when Cole swung to face him he saw that the great, square face was red, the eyes as vicious as those of a tormented rattler.

"So you didn't listen," Keldson said. "And you didn't ride."

"I listened all right," Cole said. "I just didn't ride."

The gunman moved back until he stood in the middle of the room. Cole swung a little so he could watch both of them. He was close enough to the gunman to see that his pale-blue eyes glittered with a frosty eagerness. Cole's first estimate of the little man had not been wrong. This was a killer who killed not so much for money as for pleasure.

Chairs scraped back beside the window

and poker chips cascaded to the floor from a tipped table. Turning his head, Cole saw four Chain punchers moving toward him. He was boxed on three sides — by the punchers, the gunman, and Keldson. The bar to his back completed the box.

The bar and the bartender he couldn't watch. But he was not surprised when he felt a sawed-off double barrel prod him in the side.

Eagerness crept into Keldson's eyes, the wicked eagerness of a man who likes to hurt and cripple.

No gunfight, this, Cole thought. Nothing so quick and simple as that. He'd under-estimated Keldson. He wouldn't be eating Mrs. Davis's dinner at twelve. He'd be lucky to be alive at twelve.

This wouldn't be a fight between him and Keldson, either. Sidonie had said last night that Keldson was dangerous and unpredict-able. He should have taken her words literally.

Keldson motioned toward the gunman. "Let him try for his gun, Le Clair. Let him try if he wants to. But if he does, kill him."

The shotgun prodded deeper into Cole's ribs, as though by way of warning. And Cole's mind was racing. Le Clair! Duke Le Clair! Cole had heard of him.

Keldson laughed and turning to the bar picked up a nearly empty whisky bottle.

Chuckling deep in his chest, Keldson moved slowly and confidently toward Cole, the whisky bottle raised in his right hand.

Chapter Five

When Keldson was close enough, he nodded at the bartender. "All right, Sam," and the shotgun was withdrawn. Then, while Cole watched Keldson warily, the shotgun muzzle swung, striking him squarely on the bridge of the nose.

A spurt of blood came from Cole's nose. Tears sprang to his eyes. Free of the shotgun's threat, he dropped to the floor, snatching for his gun. Keldson, however, anticipated Cole's move. His boot came out and caught Cole squarely in the face.

Cole fell in the sawdust flat on his back, and Keldson spoke to one of his men. "All right, get him," and returned the whisky bottle to the bar unused.

Cole rolled to get his hands and knees under him and to protect his belly. A boot collided with his head, and hands seized both of his arms. Struggling, he was dragged to his feet. He felt his gun lifted from its holster and heard it thump solidly on the bar top.

"Hold him," Keldson said, "I'm going to make him really wish he'd drifted."

Cole threw his head back against the face of the puncher behind him, twisting and plunging and trying to break free, kicking at Keldson who stood in front of him, and missing by a good two feet.

There were too many of them. One of Chain's punchers had an arm around his throat. Two others held him by the arms, twisting them savagely until they seemed ready to break. Sweating, Cole relaxed.

Keldson grinned and stood still, his only movement the heaving of his chest. Turning, he grabbed the soggy bar towel from where it had been dropped on the mahogany. He tore it in two with a ripping sound, and began to wind one half carefully around his right hand. When he had finished, he wound the other half around his left. He took his time, the grin never leaving his face.

Cole glanced at Le Clair. The gunman was watching, but there was an expression of distaste on his face. Contempt, too, when he looked at Marty Keldson. Duke Le Clair was a Texas gunfighter — a killer. And maybe a murderer. Yet he had his own tight code of ethics, a carryover from the Southern chivalry that had seeped west from the gulf and border states. A man fought with a gun but not with his fists because it was degrading. He never fought an enemy held helpless by others.

Le Clair turned to leave, but stopped at Keldson's order, "You stay here, Duke. You stay. I want you to see this."

Then he swung, swiftly and brutally, the towel-wrapped fist smashing Cole's lips against his teeth. His left came out, landing in Cole's stomach just below his ribs. Pain exploded from the area like the concussion waves of a charge of dynamite. Cole's head reeled, and then was snapped back by a second right from the grunting Keldson.

Cole fixed his eyes on the man. There was no fear in them, just hate, a hate so virulent that Keldson stopped momentarily.

Then a roar broke from Keldson's throat. The toweled fists came out again, smashing, cutting, closing those two eyes that had stared at him so defiantly. They smashed Cole's nose and mouth, driving him to the edge of unconsciousness. But still they came, smashing, cutting, as if Keldson were trying to beat his conscience instead of another man's face.

Cole heard someone shout, the sound

dim as though it had traveled a great distance. He thought it must have come from Duke Le Clair. He heard other shouting, and he heard the growing protests of the men who held him.

Then the first voice, this time sharp and angry, "That's enough! Damn you, Marty, I said that was enough!"

The beating stopped. Someone shoved Cole back against the bar and held him there. Another man held a beer glass half filled with whisky to his battered mouth, and poured the contents into it.

The whisky was like fire on his smashed lips, like fire in his mouth. He swallowed, and choked, and swallowed again. Then he put his hands against the bar behind him and supported himself, somehow finding enough strength in his rubberlike knees to support his weight. From half-closed eyes he glared at the men in the half circle before him.

Cole recognized the three who had held him, and the fourth who had remained aloof. He saw Duke Le Clair's shamed and angry face. He saw Keldson, sweating, his barrel chest heaving like a bellows, and he heard his ragged breathing. Then Cole saw another man with a star on his chest. Dusty Rhodes, liveryman, part time marshal and deputy sheriff.

"What's the trouble here?" Rhodes asked.

"Damned trouble-maker, this drifter," Keldson panted. "Lock him up, Dusty. When he can stand, we'll ride him out of town on a rail."

"Who started the fight?"

"He did." Keldson looked around belligerently at his men. None of them disputed his word. Even Dick Walters, standing near the door, did not voice a protest.

Rhodes turned to the bartender. "That right, Sam?"

Sam must have nodded, although Cole couldn't see him. Rhodes moved over and took his arm. "No use asking you. You'd say Keldson started it, wouldn't you?"

Cole made a grin, though it hurt his mouth to do it. He said bitterly, "Your mind's made up, ain't it, marshal? You take your orders from Chain, so you better do what the big man says."

Rhodes flushed. "Come along. You'll get twenty-four hours in jail and the Judge'll give you a ten-dollar fine for disturbing the peace. After that you can drift."

"I can, but I won't."

"Don't crowd me, son. Just come along."

Cole shrugged wearily. The prospect of twenty-four hours of quiet and lying on a bunk, even a hard one, was suddenly appealing. But before he went, he looked at Keldson and said, "You think about this, mister, because I'm going to be thinking about it."

Then he was walking beside the marshal, through the deep sawdust of the saloon and out into the bright, painful sunlight. He reeled like a drunken man as they crossed the street intersection, and when they stepped up on the boardwalk in front of the bank, he stumbled and would have fallen if it had not been for Rhodes's grip on his arm.

He found it hard to think, but there was something back there in the saloon that was queer. Then he remembered. Silence when he left, not the babble of voices which usually follows a fight. He thought with some satisfaction, *Keldon lost more today than I did. He lost the respect of his men.*

The thought did not give him as much consolation as it should have. He realized that the only thing that could fully satisfy him was Keldson's death.

"Here," Rhodes said, and opening a thick wooden door, motioned for Cole to go into the building.

Cole went in. It was a small office with a desk and two chairs and a gun rack on the wall. The air was cool, the light thin, and a moment passed before he saw Dick Walters

65

sitting in a third chair in the corner.

"What do you want?" Rhodes asked roughly.

"I've got something to tell you," Walters said. "I didn't want to say it back there in the saloon."

"Why not?" Rhodes demanded. "I was asking questions."

"You know why. Same reason you and Judge Benson and a lot of people around here don't do what they're supposed to."

"All right," Rhodes said. "What is it?"

"I was in the Staghorn when this fellow shows up asking for Andy Carew. He didn't start that ruckus. Keldson did. Sam shoved a shotgun at him." He motioned to Cole. "Then Keldson moved in and had three of his boys hold him. He didn't have no chance, Dusty."

Rhodes moved past Cole and opened a metal door. "In here, Knapp."

"Ain't you gonna do anything?" Walters demanded. "You can't hold him for disturbing the peace when he didn't —"

"I am holding him," Rhodes said, "and the charge is disturbing the peace."

Cole stumbled through the door and along the corridor and into the empty cell Rhodes indicated. He sprawled on the nearest bunk. He heard the barred door slammed shut, then Walters's dogged voice through the metal grill, "You've got to take a stand somewhere, Dusty. I told you —"

"I heard it and I'll tell Judge Benson when Knapp comes up for trial," Rhodes said. "Now you go play with your Regulators. I'm done listening."

They left. Cole was alone in the jail. He looked around at his cell. A small, barred window in the concrete wall. A metal bunk with a thin mattress and two worn, dirty blankets. A slop jar. That was all.

He dropped back on the mattress and closed his eyes. Sidonie Carew had been right about Dick Walters. He wasn't as tough as he'd wanted Cole to think last night at the stone cabin. Still, he seemed a decent kind of man.

Well, he could forget Walters. But not Marty Keldson. He'd ridden here to kill a man. Now he found himself hoping Keldson was that man. And he was pretty sure he was.

Chapter Six

Cole was roused from his stupor by the sound of the cell door clanging shut. He opened one blackened eye and stared upward from the filthy bunk.

Anger stirred in him as he heard Rhodes's voice, "You got a visitor, Knapp." After that the man's boot heels receded along the corridor and the metal door slammed shut.

Cole sat up, wincing, and rubbed at his eyes. Blood was caked on his face, and his head pounded viciously. He scowled at his visitor, aware that his anger was caused only in part by being awakened. Most of it was because his visitor's impeccable cleanliness contrasted so sharply with his own dirty, unshaven, and beaten condition.

The man held a black derby in his hand as if he were making a social call. He was tall, and slightly stooped with age. His eyes were sharp and intelligent, but not sympathetic. Rather they were the eyes you sometimes saw in a banker, Cole thought, calculating eyes that had encountered the worst in people so often they had gradually come to expect it.

"I'm Judge Benson," the man said.

"Well?"

"If you're sensible, you can get out of here in two minutes."

Cole sat up, bracing himself by putting both hands palms down against the bunk. He waited a moment until the walls of the cell quit turning, then he said, "What do you mean by being sensible? Leaving the country, maybe?"

Benson flushed, his eyes on the window above Cole's head. "To put it bluntly, yes. Andy Carew is gone. He's been gone nine years. He was probably killed in a brawl somewhere. Besides, the Carews are suspicious of you."

"You mean Keldson, don't you?"

"I'm including him. I don't blame him either. What do you expect? You're a drifter, a — a saddle bum. You ride into a country that's getting along fine and you start asking about a man who, if he were here and alive would stand to inherit half of the richest spread in the country. What's your game, Knapp?" Benson's eyes were pinned on Cole's face now. "What are you after?"

When Cole didn't answer, Benson went on, "I hear you told Dick Walters you came here to kill a man — settle with him. Who, Knapp? And why?"

"Nobody until I get out of here. You can't hold me forever on a charge of disturbing the peace and you know it."

"Then you won't leave the country?"

"No."

Benson's lips tightened. "You give me no choice, Knapp. I'll hold you under five hundred dollars' bail until I'm able to schedule your trial."

Cole grinned. "And I suppose that'll be six months from now."

"At least that. Perhaps a year." Benson's anger had been increasing until now he acted as if he couldn't remain here in the cell with Cole for another minute. He rapped on the cell bars with his gold-headed cane. "Rhodes. Get me out of here."

"You interest me, Judge," Cole said. "Do judges in this part of the country take fees for representing one side of the cases they try?"

Benson turned to glare at Cole, then swung back to the door. Rhodes unlocked the cell. "Everything all right, Judge?"

Benson didn't answer that question either. He stalked out of the jail without a word, his face red with suppressed fury. Rhodes looked at Cole plaintively. "What the hell did you say to him? He'd have got you out if you'd kept your mouth shut."

"Maybe I like it here, Dusty. Or maybe I didn't like the deal he offered."

Rhodes shrugged. Cole lay back on the bunk. He was angry now, a slow, deep anger that had its roots in injustice and helplessness. He'd made a mistake, taking on Keldson and Le Clair and the whole Chain crew. He would not make that mistake again.

He thought of Dick Walters who had failed to speak up in Cole's defense when Rhodes had arrested him in the saloon. Yet, under the circumstances, he could not blame the man. He was typical of everyone in the community who feared and hated Marty Keldson. Given a little time and leadership, Walters and others like him might be the allies Cole would need to do the job he had come here to do.

Misery and pain were deep within him. Nausea crawled in his stomach. He thought about Mrs. Davis, and the meal she had prepared for him at noon. He wondered about the bail set so high at $500, and despair became a sickness in him.

But it didn't last. There had to be a way,

and he would find it. He got up and strode to the window, ignoring his aching body and refusing to favor his injuries. Scowling, he stared into the street. As he stood there, a buggy pulled up and Sidonie stepped down. She took an iron weight from the buggy and went around to clip it to the horse's bit, then turned toward the jail door.

Cole heard her voice, the words indistinguishable, but oddly comforting to his ears. He heard Rhodes answer, then both of them crossed the office to the metal door. Rhodes unlocked it, calling, "You're bailed out, Knapp."

Cole looked at the girl as she came along the corridor. "Whose idea is this? And what are the conditions?"

"It's my idea, and there are no conditions. I'm simply repaying you for helping me last night. I don't know why you did it. But a favor is a favor, regardless of the motive."

"Suppose I skip bail?"

"I only wish you would," she said. "I don't know why you're here, but you must have proved to yourself by now that you can only cause more trouble if you stay. No, don't worry about the bail, Mr. Knapp. Chain can afford to lose it, but I'm not sure Chain can afford to have you stay."

"I won't skip bail, Miss Carew."

She looked directly at him. Suddenly she seemed to become aware of the pain that was in him. Her eyes softened as she said, "Come on. We'll stop by and see Doc Holt. If he's sober, he can patch you up."

Rhodes unlocked the cell door. Sidonie led the way out and Cole followed. He wanted a drink, but even more he wanted a bath, a shave, and clean clothes. Afterward, about twelve hours' sleep would do.

Rhodes called, "Wait a minute, Knapp." Cole stopped at the desk long enough to get his gun and hat and the odds and ends that had been in his pockets. Cole signed a receipt for them and stepped outside to where Sidonie was waiting. The sun hit him like a physical blow. He squinted against it, but not before pain shot through his head from its merciless glare. Sidonie took his arm, saying, "Upstairs over the bank. We'll see if Doc's in his office."

They climbed an outside stairway. Sidonie opened a door at the top, and they went through it and along a hall to an office in the back. The room was redolent with the smell of whisky and strong, stale cigar smoke. A roll top desk against one wall was littered with piled up papers. A swivel chair was losing its horsehair stuffing through a rent in the leather. A brass spittoon was apparently set in the wrong place, for the floor around it testified to Doc's abominably poor aim. Beside it lay an empty brown whisky bottle.

At the far side of the room a man lay on a leather-covered couch, snoring loudly. His mouth hung open, displaying discolored teeth. His jaw had felt no razor for at least two days. His skin was beaded with sweat and he tossed restlessly.

Sidonie crossed the room and shook him vigorously. "Doc! Wake up! It's Sidonie Carew."

He grunted and wheezed, but did not open his eyes. Cole said, "You're wasting your time."

"No." She shook Doc again vigorously. "I'll bring him out of it."

This time he sat bolt upright, and stared at them out of bloodshot eyes. "Whattaya want?"

Cole pushed Sidonie aside. He said, "I need some patching, Doc."

"Who're you?" Doc reached a pudgy hand to the desk and found a thick-lensed pair of glasses. He put them on and stood up, a short, untidy man in wrinkled clothes that looked as if he had slept all night in them; and that, Cole thought, was probably just what he had done. Doc peered at Cole, then

74

reached for the whisky bottle on the floor.

"Go wash your face. Them cuts will heal without no help from me. Go away." He tilted the bottle, found it empty, and threw it across the room with an exclamation of disgust. He opened a desk drawer, found another bottle, and pulling the cork, drank deeply without choking and without grimacing.

Cole looked at Sidonie. "He'd do more harm than good. Let's leave him alone."

She nodded agreement and led the way out of the office and along the hall and down the stairs. As he left the room, Cole heard the couch creak beneath Doc's bulk and an instant later there was the sound of snoring.

When they reached the street, Cole asked, "What do folks around here do when someone really needs him?"

"They sober him up," Sidonie answered. "Cold water and black coffee." She looked directly at him. "What are you going to do now?"

He stared across the street at the Staghorn. The Chain horses were gone. "What happened to your bully boys?" he asked.

She flushed. "They went back to Chain. They're branding late calves on Triangle Mesa. I asked what you were going to do now?"

"I've got a room at Mrs. Davis's. Maybe she'll patch me up and fix me a hot bath."

"I'll walk with you," she said.

"You don't need to. I won't get into any more trouble, now that your crew's out of town."

"I'm not so sure about that. You seem to have a talent for trouble."

"Perhaps," he said. "Thank you for getting me out of the calaboose. You won't be sorry. I'm not here to hurt you."

"But you are here to hurt somebody," she said. "Do you know what an opportunist is, Mr. Knapp?"

He nodded.

"I think that's what you are. Andy's dead, or he would have been back before now. Zelda believes he told you about Chain and you came here to get it. She says you'd kill anybody who gets in your way of marrying into it or whatever your scheme is. But you won't get it, Mr. Knapp. You won't get it as long as I'm here to stop you."

"And Keldson?"

"He'll stop you if I can't, in a much more unpleasant way. Good day, Mr. Knapp."

He caught her arm. "Wait. Would you believe me if I told you Andy was dead? That he'd been murdered, and I'm here to get the man who did it?"

She pulled free of his grip, a hand going up to her throat. For a long moment she stared at him, then she said, "No, I'm not sure I would."

She turned and walked away. He went slowly toward the bridge and the Davis house, realizing that Sidonie really had no reason to believe him. Andy had been gone a long time. He had never contacted his sister, never even written home. She might hate and fear Marty Keldson, but at least she knew him. As far as Chain was concerned, she doubtless trusted him. And she probably felt a strong tie to Zelda, who had practically raised her. No, he couldn't blame Sidonie. It would take time to prove to her he had no selfish motive in coming, and he wasn't sure he had that much time.

When he reached the Davis house, he knocked and Mrs. Davis opened the door. Her face showed concern the instant she looked at Cole. "Come in, Mr. Knapp. I'll get some things and patch you up."

She led the way to the kitchen. "I had a boiler of water on the stove and I thought you'd like a hot bath. Afterward you can go to bed and I'll wash your clothes." Beyond her on the kitchen floor he saw a steaming tub in front of the stove. "There's an old bathrobe on a chair. Take your time. When you get done, put the robe on and leave your clothes on the floor."

"You're very kind," he said.

"No, Mr. Knapp. I'm not kind at all. It's just that I know who did this to you. I don't know why, but that's not important. He's the only man around here capable of a thing like that. You see he beat my husband the same way about six months ago, only my husband died. I hate Keldson, Mr. Knapp, as you must hate him. Now go along. I'll patch you up when you're finished."

She closed the door and Cole undressed and crawled into the tub. He wondered what her father-in-law was like and whether he hated Keldson as she did. Suddenly he realized how lucky he was to have found this place. After what had happened, probably no one else would have given him a room.

Another thought, a disquieting one, occurred to him then. By staying here he would be endangering both Janet Davis and her father-in-law. Keldson's hate was like a prairie fire. He would destroy both Janet and Davis if by doing so he could also destroy Cole.

Then the tub's hot water and his own drowsiness crept over him. He put thoughts of Keldson out of his mind and surrendered to this pure luxury.

Chapter Seven

After leaving Cole, Sidonie walked quickly to her buggy, unhooked the cast-iron weight from the horse's bridle and tossed it into the rig. Then she stepped into the seat and took up the lines. She swung the buggy, and, turning at the main intersection, headed north on the road to Chain.

Keldson, she knew, would not be pleased when he heard she had posted Cole Knapp's bail. Nor was she particularly pleased with herself for doing so. In her direct way, she examined her own irritation and displeasure, and questioned herself about its cause.

Knapp, she decided, made an unforgettable impact upon everyone he met. Admittedly, he had come to Cedar for the purpose of killing a man. But had Andy really been murdered? Had Knapp been his friend? Was he here to kill Andy's murderer?

There was no way she could find the answers to these questions. If Andy had been killed, surely she would have been notified by the officials. Or her father, if he had been alive then. She shook her head. No, she didn't believe what Knapp had said. Any man could come here and claim he had been Andy's friend.

But why was he here? Why, unless he was the opportunist she accused him of being, playing some game which had not yet become plain. Before she was halfway to Chain, she reached the reluctant conclusion that she had made a mistake in bailing Cole out. Still, in a way she was glad. There had been no reason for Marty to beat him the way he had. And she had to admit she was drawn to Cole Knapp in a way she had never been drawn to another man.

As she climbed the steep, winding road to the mesa, she realized she was forcing her buggy horse to trot, and immediately reined in and allowed the animal a blow. Waiting, she looked down upon the town, acutely aware of its dispirited shabbiness.

She looked out across the valley, green with growing hay. A small part of it belonged to her, but the bulk of Chain's hay meadows lay north of Triangle Mesa along Coroner Creek. Her father had tried to get possession of the valley of the Big Horse in the same way that he had expanded along

Coroner Creek until he'd finally owned all of it; but here he had not succeeded, largely because of the effective leadership of young Bud Davis, the same Davis that Zelda and Marty claimed was an outlaw.

Her father was dead and Davis had been murdered. Now, even though she nominally owned Chain, too many important decisions were being made by Marty Keldson, and Marty was a man whose ambitions were endless. This was something she simply could not understand. She was satisfied with Chain exactly as it was, but her father had never been satisfied and Marty was worse.

She tried to put this out of her mind as she put all unpleasant things out of her mind if she could, things like the murder of Bud Davis. Even an outlaw, she told herself, did not deserve to be beaten to death.

She let her gaze rise to the peaks of the San Juans to the east, shrouded today by nesting clouds that obscured their eternally snow-capped peaks. The air was hot on her face, and even a transient breeze that stirred her hair brought no relief.

She watched a buck come out of the cedars below her, his four-inch horns covered with velvet. She saw a coyote slink, panting, into the cedars not far from the deer.

Her face turned soft with her thoughts, thoughts of Andy who had left the country when she was a child, of her father now dead, of the Chain she loved. Abruptly she turned and clucked to the horse. He began the climb again, this time at an unhurried walk.

Sidonie's eyes strayed back to the town and picked out the Davis house. Her mouth tightened with displeasure. What was Cole doing now? Bathing in the kitchen? Shaving? Or was Janet Davis dressing the cuts and bruises on his face with her gentle and efficient hands?

Suddenly Sidonie laughed. She was behaving exactly like a woman — almost as though she were jealous of Cole. Yet how can you be jealous of a man who is not yours, whom you have not even decided you want to be yours — a man you distrust?

The horse reached the top of the grade and Sidonie slapped his back with the lines. He broke into a trot and she drove on to the barn. When the choreman came out, she got down and let him unhitch and lead the horse away. On impulse, she called after him, "Joey, would you saddle my mare?"

"Sure, Miss Carew."

She went toward the house, somewhat at peace with herself for the first time today.

Inside, she found Zelda curled up like a kitten in her private parlor in the back of the house. She was reading a novel by Mrs. E. D. E. N. Southworth that had just arrived. She put the book down and smiled at Sidonie who dropped into a red plush chair.

"Zelda, what do you think of Cole Knapp?" Sidonie asked.

"He's uncouth, to say the least," Zelda said. "And he's been a worry to me from the moment he asked about Andy."

"Why?"

"Because he'll make trouble for us."

"How can he make trouble for Chain?"

Zelda hesitated, then reached for her book. "I told you this morning. He's got some kind of a scheme for filling his pockets at Chain's expense. He's up to something or he wouldn't have come here asking about Andy. Maybe he killed Andy. How do we know?"

Zelda started to read. Watching her, Sidonie thought there was more in her mind than she had said. She was worried about something. From years of living with her, Sidonie knew that Zelda had little real concern for anything or anyone except Marty.

Many times Zelda had bent Bill Carew to her will because of Marty. When Andy had left, Sidonie had been too young to know what was happening; now the thought occurred to her that Marty and Zelda's overweening love for him might have been responsible for Andy's leaving.

"Did you know Marty gave Cole Knapp a beating and had him thrown into jail?" Sidonie asked.

Zelda looked up from her book. "No, but it's not surprising. It's why I warned Knapp to leave the country. I know Marty. I know how he gets when he's crossed."

"Do you know what he'll do if Knapp stays?"

"Yes," Zelda said calmly. "Marty will kill him."

"The way Bud Davis was killed?"

"Perhaps, but you mustn't be too hard on Marty. He's like your father, Sidonie. You and Chain are his life. He'll do anything to protect you or the ranch."

For a moment Sidonie stared at Zelda, shocked by the lack of emotion in Zelda's voice. Then she got up and strode from the room. She went upstairs and changed to her riding skirt and blouse. She came downstairs again and went out through the front door. Her mare stood saddled beside the barn, nuzzling grain spilled on the ground.

She mounted and rode out of the yard,

and for a few moments let the mare run free, as though the rushing air could blow the troubled thoughts from her mind. When the mare slowed, Sidonie made no effort to guide the animal but let her pick her own way across the mesa.

This was rolling country that lay between Coroner Creek on the north and Big Horse which bordered Triangle Mesa on the east and south. The tableland was occasionally broken by rocky outcroppings or by ridges covered by cedars and piñons, giving cows and calves protection from the icy spring storms that swept the mesa. Eastward the land rose in gradual stages until it reached the far peaks of the San Juan range.

Everywhere Sidonie saw Chain cattle, fat and sleek already. The grass was green and fresh, despite the lack of rain this spring. It seemed to Sidonie that there were hundreds of new calves, running and frolicking, their tails small flags in the wind.

Most of the calves were already branded. But she knew that, even now, Marty and his Chain crew were out here gathering stragglers, branding late calves and those that had escaped branding during spring roundup.

She came upon them unexpectedly as she rode over a long rise, and she reined in instantly while still shielded by cedars. There she sat watching.

Below her the riders had gathered perhaps two hundred cattle. Part of the crew sat their horses in a circle around the herd, lounging indolently in their saddles. Three others rode slowly and watchfully through the herd, and every now and then a rope would go out and a bawling calf would be dragged from the bunched cattle. Not far behind always came the calf's mother, bellowing menacingly but ineffectively.

Dust raised as the calf was dragged to the fire. Here one of Chain's dismounted crewmen would seize it and throw it on its side. Two men held while a third ran from the fire, branding iron in hand. Smoke rose briefly from the calf's hip, the blue smoke of burning hair. And back to the fire went the man with the iron.

Now another man earmarked, altered, and dehorned. Another with a hypodermic syringe vaccinated against blackleg. Then the calf was up, shaken, outraged, but with only temporary hurt. A slap on the flank sent him scurrying back to the herd, and behind him came his still bawling mother to lick his head and assure herself he was not injured.

Another calf was dragged from the herd,

and another. Now and then one of the crew would cut out a grown animal from the herd, one that had not been dehorned, or needed doctoring for some kind of injury. When this happened, two men would put their ropes on him, one around the neck, the other around one or both hind feet.

Horses, backing, would stretch the animal out until it fell. Then the men moved in, quick and sure, impersonal as surgeons with their knives and dehorning saws.

This was an old and familiar scene to Sidonie, and one that she loved to watch. She took pride in it, too. Chain was an efficient ranch, well managed by Marty and his crew, in the same way as old Bill Carew had worked the outfit. Whatever Marty's faults were, and by Sidonie's standards they were many, laziness was not among them. Or inefficiency. Chain would grow under his direction and prosper.

The growing was what bothered Sidonie. Under Marty Keldson Chain would be like a fungus, never staying the same, never shrinking. It would spread like an oil stain on water until every settler along the Big Horse had been crowded out, perhaps even until the town of Cedar was gone. She'd heard Marty say Chain had no need of a town this close. But regardless of what happened to the town, the growing wouldn't stop. It would go on until it would crowd even the ranchers on its borders.

Unless it was stopped. Unless Keldson was stopped.

Sidonie's mare had moved out of the cedars, grazing. Suddenly Keldson looked up from below, saw her, and loped his horse up the slope toward her.

Reaching her, Keldson's voice was rough. "What're you doing here, Sid?"

The tone irritated her as it always did when he used it on her. She said, "Chain's mine. I'll watch what I please."

"Not after —" He stopped, a suggestion of embarrassment coming over his heavy, square face.

Sidonie finished, "After we're married? You're jumping to conclusions, Marty. I haven't said I'd marry you."

He looked at her sharply. "What do you want from a man, Sid? You know I'll look after you — protect you and everything that belongs to you. Is it pretty words you want? Courtin'? I ain't much of a hand at them things. You know how I feel though. You know."

"Do I?" she asked sweetly, hating herself for her deliberate sweetness. "How could I know? You never told me."

He had a soft side. On rare occasions he had shown it to her, and many times she had seen it when he was with his mother. But he seemed to be ashamed of it. It was the other side he was proud of — his brutality, his ruthlessness, the driving way he had of getting things done. Now he seemed caught in the confusion she had aroused in him.

"All right," he said helplessly. "I'll tell you. I —"

"Never mind," Sidonie said sharply. "There's something else I wanted to talk to you about. You beat Cole Knapp and had him thrown into jail. Why?"

"You know why," Keldson said. "He's a damned trouble-maker. He asked for what he got."

"Did he ask three of your men to hold him while you beat him half to death? I just wanted you to know the Judge held him for five hundred dollars and I put up the bail. He's free."

Keldson's face was like a thundercloud. "Why'n hell —"

"Don't swear at me, Marty," Sidonie said quietly.

"I wasn't. But why'n hell —"

Sidonie's voice was soft, but it was penetrating and steady. "I did it to show you something, Marty. You can run Chain, at least as long as Dad's will lets Zelda control it, but you aren't going to decide its policy. What you did today reflects on Chain and it's got to stop. Do I make myself clear?"

"Yeah, clear as mud. I'll tell you why you bailed that drifter out if you don't know yourself. You're in love with him."

Sidonie stared at him, felt her face flush, then suddenly could not meet Keldson's contemptuous gaze. She said coldly, "You're Zelda's son, so you have some rights on Chain. But don't overstep them. Don't overstep them again."

She forced herself to meet his gaze. She saw something in his eyes, something half hidden, and could not have said exactly what it was. But it made her afraid and cold inside. Angrily she whirled the mare and set the spurs in her sides. She rode away at a hard run and did not look back.

Chapter Eight

Cole slept the clock around, occasionally moaning in his sleep. In full daylight he came awake suddenly, startled and uneasy as his opening eyes fell upon unfamiliar surroundings. Then he heard dishes rattle in the kitchen, smelled coffee and frying bacon, and relaxed as he remembered where he was.

He threw back the blanket and sat up. His head reeled and the room swam in front of him, but he had his feet on the floor now and would not give up. For a time he remained motionless, head tipped forward, eyes closed, hands fisted at his sides.

From the waist up his body was one great throbbing ache. Keldson's fists, and the hands of the men who had held Cole's twisted arms behind his back had done their work well.

Suddenly a vast impatience was in him. Sitting here on the edge of the bed nursing his aches and pains would accomplish nothing. He stood up and grabbed the brass knob atop one of the bedposts until the waves of nausea passed. When he could, he shook his head in disgust, for he knew that today would be lost.

Irritation grew in him as he looked around for his clothes and failed to find them. He released his hold on the bedpost and crossed the room, the exertion bringing a fine film of sweat to his face. He opened the door a crack and called, "Mrs. Davis, what did you do with my clothes?"

"I'll bring them right away, Mr. Knapp." Her voice was pleasant, cheerful, and good to hear. In a lower tone she said, "Watch the bacon, Dad. Don't let it burn, you hear?" Then her steps came through the kitchen door and across the parlor. She said, "Get back into bed, Mr. Knapp."

Stubbornly he put his hand through the crack in the door. "Just give me my clothes."

"No, I'm coming in," she said firmly. "You're a badly beaten man, Mr. Knapp. If you stay in this community, you need to get well, and quickly. Are you going to stay?"

"I'll stay, all right."

"Then don't leave this house until you feel like fighting because that's probably what you'll have to do." She stood on the other side of the door, waiting. "I have some liniment and I want to rub you with it several times today. If you're like my husband was, the soreness won't be gone for quite a while."

Cole remained where he was, irritation growing in him. He'd rented a room and arranged for meals, but nursing and rubdowns hadn't been part of the deal. Like an injured wolf, he wanted only to be off by himself. Or to fight again those who had hurt him.

There was tartness in her voice when she spoke again. "Modesty is fine in its place, Mr. Knapp, but it's hardly worth dying for. If you go out now, that's exactly what you'll do. I know what I'm talking about, believe me."

She sounded like a determined woman, and Cole knew the quickest way to get his clothes and breakfast was to let her do as she wished. He closed the door, and returning to the bed, pulled the blanket up to his neck. He called, "All right."

She came in and laid his clothes, carefully folded, on the foot of the bed, then moved around to the side and set the bottle of liniment on the stand. "Your clothes are washed and ironed," she said impersonally. "I darned your socks and sewed up the rip down the back of your shirt, but I'm afraid it will tear again when you put it on."

"I'll buy some new clothes today."

"Not today and probably not tomorrow." She folded the blanket back to his waist. He clutched at it and tried to pull it back, but she stopped him with her words, "I am not a girl, Mr. Knapp. Just look at yourself. You're a solid, purple bruise from your waist to your neck."

She poured liniment into a cupped palm and began to rub, first his chest, then his shoulders and arms, and finally his stomach and ribs. Her strong hands moved in a circular pattern, leaving a warm glow wherever they worked. When she finished she said, "Turn over. I'll do your back."

He obeyed, his irritation gone. She knew what she was doing, and he seemed to heal under her hands. He relaxed, closing his eyes and surrendering at last to this unexpected but welcome luxury.

"Why are you doing this?" he asked.

"I'll do anything and everything I can to save your life. If I didn't take care of you the soreness wouldn't leave your body for days. After you've eaten I'll heat some bricks and send you back to bed with them. The combination of heat, liniment, and massage should do wonders for you. Tonight I'll fix you another hot bath."

She stepped back and corked the liniment bottle. She wiped her hands on her apron, and took a small jar from its pocket. "Put some of this salve on your face. Breakfast will be ready in five minutes."

She left the room, closing the door behind her. Cole daubed salve gingerly on his cheeks and jaws where Keldson's fists had bruised and battered them. His lips were swollen and split, his nose sore. Neither eye would open fully, but all of these were minor injuries that time would heal.

He dressed, pleasantly aware of the lessened pain in his body, and thinking it had been a long time since his clothes had been clean. He'd been on the trail almost a month, with time for nothing but eating, sleeping, and riding. Now that he was here, the prodding sense of urgency was gone. He'd built a fire under Keldson and could afford to wait a bit, providing he stayed alive that long.

When he went into the kitchen, Mrs. Davis was frying eggs at the stove. A little man at the table got up, and as he held out his hand, Cole noticed that all the fingers were missing save for the index finger and thumb. He gripped the hand, finding the palm hard with calluses.

The little man said, "I'm Ben Davis,

Janet's father-in-law." He grinned in a friendly way as Cole sat down. "Like to see you tangle with Keldson sometime when you've got both arms free. Might be a different story."

"You'll see it," Cole said.

He instinctively liked Davis. The little man couldn't stand over five feet five or six, and Cole doubted if he weighed one hundred and fifteen pounds soaking wet; but size, as far as Cole was concerned, was not a measure of a man's worth. Ben Davis had a look of toughness about him like a dry spruce knot. Anyone who tangled with him, Cole thought, would find they'd tied into a pan-size buzz saw.

Davis eyed Cole with equal interest. He said, "Sure admire a man with guts enough to tackle Keldson. Don't know what you've got agin' him, but just bein' agin' him puts me on your side."

Cole grinned, the pain of his split lips making him grimace. He said, "Judging from what happened yesterday, looks like I'll need someone on my side."

"Stay alive and you'll have more friends," Davis said. "Take my word for it. Give Keldson's cussedness time to pile up and some of 'em that are too scared to holler right now will give you a hand." He shook his head. "I dunno, though. You'll have to work at gettin' 'em over bein' scared, and that ain't gonna' be easy, even if you do stay alive."

Janet moved from the stove with the skillet and lifted the eggs carefully onto Cole's and Davis's plates. She returned to the stove and came back with the coffeepot.

Davis began to eat hungrily, but Cole waited until Janet was seated. Davis kept eyeing him even as he chewed. After a while he said, his curiosity showing in his eyes, "You've cut yourself a man-sized bite, Knapp. Everybody knows you've been askin' around for Andy Carew. They know Keldson's hell-bent on runnin' you out of the country. They're commencin' to wonder why."

Davis sat with his head cocked to one side, his eyes as bright and sparkling as a chipmunk's. His fork was poised in his hand.

"I can't tell you that," Cole said. "Not now."

"All right. Makes me no never mind. Reckon you've got your reasons. But there's a thing or two you ought to know. Everybody hereabouts but me'n Janet are scared to death of Keldson, or else toadyin' to him because Chain can do 'em good money-wise."

Janet broke in. "We're not brave, Mr. Knapp. We're afraid of Keldson, too. But Dad and I have reached the point where nothing is important any more except seeing justice done." She was silent a moment, her dark eyes troubled. Then she went on. "My husband and I had a small ranch about five miles from town on Big Horse Creek. Keldson beat my husband up just the way he did you and told him to leave the country. But Bud wasn't a man to run. Next time they caught him they killed him. They beat him so badly he died."

Angrily, Davis jabbed a fork in Cole's direction. "Same thing will happen to you next time if you ain't careful — a sight more careful than you was when you walked into that hornets' nest in the Staghorn."

Remembering Walters, Cole asked abruptly, "What about this bunch that calls themselves the Regulators?"

Davis was suddenly contemptuous. "Spit'n talk boys. Dick Walters heads 'em, now that Bud's gone, but Dick don't do nothin' but call meetin's and talk. Give 'em a few more weeks an' they'll all sell out to Keldson."

"Bud was president of the Regulators when he was alive," Janet said. "They amounted to something then, and that's

98

why Keldson killed him. Now there's nobody to fill Bud's boots. Nobody." Her voice, filled with contempt, was a tribute to her dead husband.

Davis said slyly, not looking at Cole, "Unless you do it."

Cole ignored the remark. It would be ungrateful to suggest they were concerned about him more as a tool than as a man, though at the moment it looked that way. He asked, "What's riding Keldson?"

"He's a damned land-hungry pirate, that's what." Davis pushed his chair back and tilted it. "You take the old days, when Andy was still around. Bill Carew was hard workin' and tougher'n a boot. But you couldn't help likin' him. He spread out, and he put the squeeze on anybody who got in his way, but he wasn't mean like Keldson. Change came, I reckon, when Andy's ma died. Bill married this Zelda woman, an' she wasn't no better'n she is now. Stage dancer, I hear, who didn't wear much more'n a smile when she danced. She fetched Marty, Marty bein' her boy. But Andy and Marty couldn't get along for love nor money, an' Zelda kep' takin' Marty's side. Finally Andy pulled out, an' by the Lord Harry, I don't blame him. I'd a pulled out, too."

"When Bill died," Janet said, "everybody

expected Andy to show up. Judge Benson put a detective on his trail, but he never came back. Nobody knows whether the detective found him or not, but I guess he didn't. If he'd found Andy, or if Andy read in the papers about his father's death, he'd have come, wouldn't he?"

"You'd think so," Cole said.

Davis jabbed his fork in Cole's direction again, impatiently. "What happened to Andy ain't no concern of ours. But what happens to us an' to Janet's child is. And I'll tell you somethin' else. I ain't goin' to rest till I square up for Bud."

"What about Bill Carew?" Cole asked. "I mean after he married Zelda."

"He began to get mean, too," Davis said, "even toward Andy, his own kid. When Marty got older Bill just let him do as he damned pleased. Even hired that gunslinger Le Clair on Marty's say so. I reckon you seen Le Clair in the Staghorn."

Cole nodded, and Davis went on disgustedly. "They make a pair if I ever seen one. Reckon it's plain enough why folks don't fight 'em."

"It's plain, all right," Cole said.

Davis finished and got up. "Well, sittin' here jawin' ain't earnin' the baby shoes." He looked at Janet with a tenderness that surprised Cole. His voice was determined, though Cole thought he detected a note of helplessness, almost desperation, in it. "That baby's goin' to have everything he needs — more'n any other baby on the Big Horse."

Janet smiled. "I'm not worried, Dad. And I doubt if the baby is."

Davis picked up a pair of pitch-covered gloves and a hat liberally sprinkled with sawdust. "I'm worried, if you ain't." He turned his gaze to Cole. "I make my livin' sellin' firewood. Got a steam-powered saw and a couple of teams to skid cedar off the hill. Trouble is, I need a man to help and can't get one. Keldson's passed the word, and when that happens nobody will touch you with a ten-foot pole. Nobody."

"I'll help you when some of this stiffness goes out of me."

"Thanks," Davis said, and there was real appreciation in his voice. "But I won't stand for it less'n I have to. You keep your shootin' hand in shape." He held out his own disfigured hand for Cole to see. "You wouldn't be fightin' Keldson with a hand like this."

He bobbed his head at Janet and went out through the back door. Then he turned and stuck it back through again, grinning. "Do what Janet says, hear? It'll be a sight easier that way. I know."

Janet brought the coffeepot from the stove and refilled Cole's cup. She said, "I knew he'd been worrying, although he hasn't said so before. Folks aren't buying wood from him like they used to. Dad keeps hauling and sawing, but it just piles up in his wood yard. That's part of what he meant by saying Keldson had passed the word."

Cole felt a deep anger inside him. "Keldson beats you up, or Le Clair shoots you, or they take your business away from you. Is that it?"

"That's about it." Her eyes were troubled again. "Keldson is a mad dog, Mr. Knapp. You've seen Dusty Rhodes, so you know what the law is. But I think Dad's wrong when he says Keldson is land hungry. It's more than that."

"What do you mean?"

"I'm not sure." She turned to the stove, moistened a finger and touched one of the bricks. "These are hot now. Go back to bed. I'll wrap them and bring them to you."

He finished his coffee and rose. "I can't stay here, Mrs. Davis."

She turned to him, anxiety shadowing her face. "Wasn't the bed comfortable? Wasn't the breakfast good?"

"I didn't mean that. But I'll bring more

trouble down on you if I stay."

"We need the money, Mr. Knapp. Every cent we can get. Her flushed face told him how hard it was for her to say the words. "As for trouble, there is nothing more Keldson can do to us now, after murdering my husband. Nothing. I — I wish you'd stay."

"All right," he said gently. "If you want me to stay I will." And he went on into his room.

Chapter Nine

Cole's battered body was slow to heal in spite of the care Janet gave him. He stayed in the house for two days, and on the third did nothing except work half an hour in the garden. Later in the day he shaved, being careful to avoid the scabs on his cheeks and jaws.

Cole's right side gave him the most trouble, grabbing him every time he drew a long breath. Janet thought he had a broken rib, but Ben Davis didn't agree. "You just got a hell of a beatin', boy," he had said out in the garden, "but you was lucky at that. I never want to see you in the shape Bud was when we brought him home. His face was bunged up so bad I wouldn't let 'em open the coffin."

"How did Janet take it?" Cole asked. "Seeing him that way, I mean?"

"Better'n I did. Seemed to, anyway. But who knows what goes on inside a woman's head." Davis's knotty fists balled at his sides. "What I keep thinkin' about is the baby. What if it marked him for Janet to see Bud like he was?" He was silent a moment, his jaw thrust out. "Know what I'll do if it did? I'll take a shotgun and go huntin' Keldson. I'll blow his head off. Then that Zelda woman can look at what's left and think of my boy."

Davis turned and walked away.

In the three days Cole had been in this home he had learned to like and respect Janet and her father-in-law. They appeared to have stood Bud's death better than most people would. Now, he knew, they both lived with memories, with the hope the baby would be a boy and look like Bud.

Not much to have left, Cole thought, when you're young and have lost your husband, when you're old and have lost your only son. Yet they had something else, too. Both lived for the day Marty Keldson would be punished, when Bud's death would be avenged. This was particularly true with Davis.

"I'm goin' to live till Keldson's dead," he said once. "After that I don't give a hang, except I do worry about how Janet will live. I don't have no money to leave her. All I got is this house and my sawin' rig. An' Bud sure didn't leave her nothin'. His ranch was mortgaged so heavy the bank took it after he died. Your bein' here helps, though. Keldson's a damn bull of a man. I don't figure he's got much sand in his craw, but maybe he's more dangerous than if he did. He's smart like a coyote. You never know what he's goin' to do."

On the morning of the fourth day Cole announced at breakfast that he couldn't stay idle any longer. He had to get out, and he wanted to see Judge Benson.

"How's your gun hand?" Davis asked.

"All right, except that my shoulder's stiff."

"Be careful. If Le Clair jumps you, you're dead." He gazed thoughtfully at Cole. "Likely you'll be all right. I doubt Le Clair will bother you. It'd be a little too plain Keldson was behind it if he did. But you'd better not ride away from town. Nobody can pin anything on a bushwhacker nobody's seen."

"I want to see Sidonie Carew. Does she come to town very often?"

"No, she doesn't," Janet said, "and you can't go to Chain. They'd kill you."

"I thought maybe I could see her without going there," Cole said. "What does she do all day? She doesn't strike me as a girl who would stay inside."

"She rides, mostly on Triangle Mesa," Janet said reluctantly, "but that's a dangerous place for you. Don't go there, Cole. Please."

"I didn't come here to stay out of trouble," he said. "I'll be all right."

He went to his room, buckled on his gun belt, and, putting on his hat went out into the harsh sunlight.

The hour was early, the streets deserted, but he found judge Benson in his office over the bank, a long cigar in his mouth. He was just as immaculate as he had been when he'd visited Cole in jail, but the calm, self-assurance that had been so much a part of him that day was missing. His nervous gaze touched the gun on Cole's hip, then raised to Cole's face.

"So you're still here. I thought you'd be gone by now."

Cole smiled. "Judge, you knew I was still around. You also know I don't intend to leave." He sat down without being invited to do so, straddling a straight-backed chair and resting his arms on its back. "Funny thing about this country, Judge — everything moving along fine and dandy till I showed up. What'd I do to upset things?"

"Nothing. You give yourself too much credit, Knapp."

"I don't think so. You're worried. You can't keep it out of your face. Maybe you're wondering if you're on the right side. Maybe you're thinking that between me and Ben Davis and Bud's widow the Regulators could be revived, put back on their feet the way they were before Keldson killed Bud."

"I'm busy, Knapp. If —"

Cole interrupted. "Or was it the question I asked about Andy Carew that started you worrying? What are you hiding, Judge?"

"Damn it, I'm not hiding anything." There was anger in Benson's voice. "There's nothing funny about the way you've been treated here. You're a trouble-maker and nobody likes a trouble-maker. It's that simple. Personally, I think Sidonie should have left you in jail."

"I'll bet you do," Cole said. "I've been wondering about Sidonie. She ain't like Marty Keldson or his mother. I'd say she's got some notions about right and wrong. Bill Carew must have planted them in her when she was a girl. Or maybe it was her mother."

The Judge's voice showed an exaggerated patience. "What do you want, Knapp? Information about Andy Carew? I can't give it to you. I don't know where he is."

"I'm not here for that. You were Bill Carew's lawyer, from what I hear. I want to know about Bill's will."

The cigar had gone cold in Benson's hand. He relighted it, taking his time and filling the office with clouds of blue smoke. His sharp eyes studied Cole the way a banker would study collateral for a loan.

Cole knew he could refuse to talk. He also knew the will was a matter of public record, available to anyone who could find where the record of it was kept.

"You'll find out anyway so I might as well tell you," the judge said wearily. "The will left all of Bill's cash money to his widow, and it was a sizable amount. I was his lawyer but I was his friend, too. He talked to me as a friend. He left Zelda the money because he thought she'd move back to Denver. She was never happy here, and Bill knew it, though he did everything he could to satisfy her. For some reason — her background, I suppose — the women of the community didn't take to her. They never called on her and they didn't invite her to join their club. They never even asked her to come to church."

When he paused, Cole said, "Go on."

"I tried through my wife to make them accept her. But a man is never more helpless than when he tries to buck a bunch of stubborn women."

"Who got Chain?"

"Andy and Sidonie, share and share alike. Andy was given a year to claim his half. If he doesn't show up in that time, the outfit, lock, stock and barrel, goes to Sidonie. Until the year's up, Zelda's responsible for its management."

"You reckon she'll leave at the end of the year?" Cole asked.

"Depends. She wants to see Marty and Sidonie married. If that happens, she'll stay. Otherwise, she'll go." He rose. "Now if you'll excuse me —"

"Sure." Cole got up, too. "You say you were Bill Carew's friend. If you were, you're Sidonie's friend, and if you're that you'll do something to bust up this marriage notion. I haven't known Marty Keldson long, but it's been long enough to know that nothing could be worse for Sidonie than marrying him."

Benson fumbled in the pocket of his vest for a match. His eyes at last met Cole's. "What's your interest in Andy and Sidonie Carew? You bucking for a slice of Chain yourself?"

Cole grinned. "That's what everybody else thinks. Why not you?" He went to the door and opened it, then turned and stared at Benson. "What are you bucking for, Judge?"

"Get out of here."

"You're riding a tough bronc, Judge. I think you're wishing to hell you were off. But you don't know how to get off without breaking your neck, do you?" He stepped into the hall and closed the door behind him. Standing there he could almost feel, even through the door, the Judge's fury, the same fury that had been in him that afternoon in the jail.

Cole went down the outside stairway and crossed the still deserted street to the livery stable. Benson was the one man in town, Cole thought, who could help if he could be goaded into it. Then he shrugged. Perhaps Benson was honest only by surface standards. Or perhaps he was afraid. In either case he'd be no good to Cole. Or Sidonie either.

Dusty Rhodes was silent until Cole's horse was saddled. Then he asked hopefully, "Pulling out?"

Cole grinned. "No such luck."

"Keep riding, man," Rhodes said. "Damn it, can't you get it through your thick skull that this town don't cotton to tough, trouble-

111

making drifters? You stay and you'll get hurt."

"Or maybe you will if you don't get rid of me. Is that what Keldson told you?"

"Go to hell," Rhodes muttered, and turned his back.

The horse had been on hay and grain for four days and nights. He'd been standing in his stall all day. Cole eyed his bunched muscles, then swung with something like anticipation into the saddle.

His side hurt with every plunge of the bucking horse, but Cole let him have it out, then struck upstream from the town, letting the horse work the kinks out of his unused muscles at a run.

A mile from Cedar, Cole found a place to climb to the mesa. When he reached the top, he angled through the cedar and piñon toward Chain's buildings, but he stopped just below the crest of a ridge while still half a mile from the house.

Patiently, now, he waited, hoping to catch Sidonie as she left. The day dragged, a litter of cigarette stubs growing around Cole's feet. Half a dozen times he almost gave up. But it was pleasant sitting with his back to a tree. The air was clear and warm, the smell of cedar good in his nostrils.

And so he stayed until in late afternoon he saw her, alone, her long shadow moving on the ground beside her.

She was too close to Chain to hail, so he only watched. She rode well, he thought. Probably she had spent the whole day on the range, riding to escape being in the house, to escape her stepmother and the lavish oak paneling and potted palms and everything else in that great, sprawling stone monument to Zelda Carew's ambitious whims.

When Sidonie disappeared, Cole rode back to town, thinking of the girl and what lay ahead for her. Surely she must hate the grossness of Marty Keldson. And yet many women, Cole knew, married men they hated.

Somehow he'd find a way to help her, as he'd promised Andy he would do. And while he waited, his battered body would be healing. Perhaps, too, he could get hold of Dick Walters and find some way to revive the Regulators.

When he reached town, he reined into the livery stable. He was surprised to see Dusty Rhodes hurrying toward him. The deputy seldom hurried. When Cole stepped down, he saw the expression of triumph on the man's weak face.

Like a boy carrying tales, Rhodes chortled. "By golly, Knapp, I warned you. But no, you knew it all. Now you're a dead man."

"Don't feel dead."

"You will. You will."

Deliberately Cole rolled a cigarette. Rhodes nearly jumped up and down with his excitement. "A gunslinger hit town this afternoon looking for you. Described you and called you by name. You're his man, all right."

"What'd he look like?"

"Shorter'n you. Thinner. Pair of eyes like a fish, and a gun tied low down on his leg. Cutaway holster. Know him now?"

Cole sighed wearily. He said, "No, I don't know him."

He wheeled toward the archway and the street. This, then, was Keldson's move. He could have used Le Clair, but that would have been too plain even to the people of Cedar, so he had brought in a killer.

If you had money, you could hire a gun. The more money you had, the faster the gun you could hire. Cole had an idea this gun would be very fast; for if Keldson didn't have enough money of his own, he could easily borrow more from his mother.

As he stepped into the street, there was an odd tightness in all of Cole's muscles. Whoever the gunman was, he wouldn't have to hunt for Cole.

He moved into the street, his gaze on the batwings of the Staghorn.

Chapter Ten

Cole Knapp was a product of desert country, that fierce and nearly empty land that was Arizona on one side of the border, Sonora on the other. It was a land of deep-rooted plant life, of saguaro, yucca, and manzanita. In its dry, merciless heat only the hardy could survive. This was true of men as well as plants.

From necessity, men grew weary in that raw land and were slow to trust a stranger. The trusting ones died young; the others lived because they had learned to fight, with knives, with guns, with whatever came to hand.

Well, Cole had survived, but his best friend hadn't. And Andy's death would not go unavenged, Cole told himself. Marty Keldson would not escape simply because he had the money to hire a killer.

Cole's face hardened as he stood there in the street, his eyes on the Staghorn. He was aware of Dusty Rhodes watching from the stable door, and he could see in his mind the expression of gleeful anticipation Rhodes was wearing. The deputy would be hoping he'd die under the stranger's gun. So would Keldson, and probably everyone else in town except Ben and Janet Davis.

A man stepped out of the Staghorn. Watching him, Cole smiled grimly. There were no secrets in a small town. A man waited, and another rode in, and within minutes both knew the other was there.

Cole had never seen this man before, but the other could not admit it. He would have a story, of a wrong done by Cole Knapp, of pursuing Cole to right that wrong. But it was hard to tell what the story would be.

The stranger moved into the street and turned to face Cole. Still watching him, Cole loosened his gun in its holster. He faced the dying sun, a disadvantage, and tugged his hat brim lower to shield his eyes from the slanting rays. He had to get this over, he thought, before the sun dropped any lower, and he began walking toward the man with even, measured steps.

The injustice of the situation angered him, but he had no regrets, either about the life he might take or the fact that the man was a total stranger. Men who hired their guns ran the chance of being killed for their pay and Cole would waste no pity on this one.

But if Cole should fail, Andy would go unavenged, and it was this that bothered him. He flexed his right shoulder, giving it a circular motion, and felt no pain. He was briefly grateful to Janet for her faithful liniment massage.

The gunman stood spread-legged in midstreet. An odd tension was in the man, tension Cole had seen before in other men at other times. "Knapp!" the gunman called. "You hear me now? It's been a long time. I reckon you knew I'd find you sooner or later, so you quit running."

"What's the story?" Cole asked wearily. "It must be a good one. You ain't about to admit you were hired to kill me."

"Hired?" The man feigned his surprise well. "Nobody hired me, Knapp. You know that as well as I do." He turned his head toward the crowd that had gathered in front of the Staghorn. "He's got reason for saying I was hired, but he's lying. I had a sister. I followed this Knapp an' her for a thousand miles. After I found her grave I followed Knapp. Now I've got him because he's tired of running."

That was the story, simple and believable. The murmur of indignation that rose from the crowd told Cole they believed it — or wanted to. Whatever the outcome of the impending gunfight, the story would be all over the country by sunup.

Cole's face darkened with anger. "You're a liar!" he shouted. "You never followed me a mile and as far as I know, you never had a sister. Keldson's blood money is in your pocket right now."

The gunman was hardly more than a youngster, tall and slender, with a week's growth of downy blond whiskers on his face attesting to the fact that he'd been on the trail for days. He looked the part of an outraged brother. More than that, he acted the part and he'd be believed.

But Cole saw something else in him. He saw the lust to kill in his eyes; he saw the predatory set of the thin mouth. He saw swagger and pride in speed and ability; he saw assurance and no fear at all.

The gunman moved forward like a stalking panther, right hand splayed near the butt of his tied-down gun. He said, without taking his eyes from Cole, "Any fool can call another man a liar. Thing is, everybody here knows I'm not."

Cole asked unexpectedly, "How old are you?" and the question brought a flush to the gunman's face, a little more wildness into his eyes. Crowding, Cole went on, "That's far enough. Stand still, sonny, and tell the folks you lied. Tell 'em Keldson hired you to kill me. Tell 'em that and I'll let you go. Then you go find Keldson and tell him not to send a boy to do a man's job."

There was no more talk in the gunman. Only blind fury remained. Cole had touched his one raw spot deliberately. Cole felt his nerves and muscles go even tighter with the waiting.

The gunman's hand closed on the butt of his gun. As the gun came out, his thumb flipped back the hammer, and the barrel began to rise.

Cole's arm, hand and shoulder moved with easy, practiced grace. His gun was level before the sights of the gunfighter's had raised above Cole's knees. His border training took over, and his bullet smashed into the man's chest and drove him back. Cole's second bullet caught him above the heart before he could fall.

Cole swung his head to look at Rhodes who still stood in the stable door. "What are your orders now, deputy?" he said bitterly. "Didn't Keldson give you any? Didn't he tell you to go through the gunman's clothes and get his money back? Or was he so sure I'd be dead that he didn't think of that?"

Rhodes was white, and he backed up a step. Cole turned to Judge Benson standing in the crowd before the saloon. "You saw it, Judge. What's the verdict?"

"Self defense," Benson said reluctantly. "The deceased drew first." He stepped into the street and looked down briefly at the gunman's face, then swung his glance to Cole. "What do you want, Knapp? More dead men in the streets of Cedar?"

Cole said, "At least one more. Maybe two. Dead men ain't anything new in Cedar, are they? What about Bud Davis?"

"Nobody knew who did it," Benson said quickly. "If we'd known, we'd have made him pay."

"Would you, Judge?" He was rewarded by the flush of shame that rose in Benson's cheeks, by the anger that glittered in his eyes.

Like buzzards attracted to carrion, the men in front of the saloon edged into the street and gathered around the dead gunfighter to look down at him. Cole holstered his gun and turned toward the bridge, suddenly tired, suddenly discouraged.

This, he knew, was only the beginning. He'd come here to stir up trouble in the hopes that Andy's killer would incriminate himself. This hired killer had convinced him that Keldson was guilty, though he had had little doubt about that from the first. But he felt sure Keldson had not killed Andy himself. So there were two that would pay with their lives, Keldson and another. Le Clair . . . ?

He wondered what effect tonight's incident would have on his own life here in Cedar. Many of the townspeople would believe the story. His thoughts turned to Sidonie. If she believed, she would naturally align herself more firmly with Keldson and Zelda, accepting their claim that Cole was an opportunist and self-seeker. If she did, Cole would become even more of an outsider, and his chances of staying alive long enough to settle with Andy's killer would be greatly reduced.

He wished now that he'd told Sidonie that first night why he was here. But he had not been sure of her, or that she'd not run to Keldson and repeat whatever he told her.

Tomorrow he had to see her. He had to get to her somehow before the story of the gunfighter's death reached her or soon after. He had to convince her that the story he'd told her the day Keldson had beaten him up was true. He had to convince her that Andy was dead and that he was here to avenge him.

Sidonie could not actively help him. Marty had too firm a grip on Chain already for that. But her belief in Cole would give him a status in the country that would help him with everybody else.

When Cole went into the Davis house, Janet called, "Supper's ready, Mr. Knapp."

Davis was on the back porch scrubbing pitch off his hands. As Cole came out to wash, Davis said, "How do you feel, son? Low? Killin' always does that to a man. I can remember when killin' a deer made me feel that way."

Cole said bitterly, "I never saw him before in my life, and I never traveled a thousand miles with any woman, his sister or anyone else."

Davis punched him in the ribs. "Hold on, son. You don't never have to convince me."

"How about the others? They'll want to believe."

"Sure. Marty coppered his bet real well. An' the story'll hurt you even if it ain't true." Davis turned toward the door. "Reckon supper's gettin' cold." He swung around as though suddenly having an unexpected thought. "Say, let's me'n you hike down to the wood yard after supper. I want you to see my steam rig. Got a whistle on it, by

122

grab, just like a locomotive. You can hear it clean up the valley to Walters's place."

Cole said, "I'd like to," and went inside. He knew what Davis was trying to do: make him forget the dead face looking up from the dusty street, make him forget the damaging story the gunman had told before he died.

Supper was an awkward meal. Janet's glances and encouraging smiles told Cole she had heard the story, too, that she didn't believe it any more than Davis had.

He was grateful for their trust, but he had to grin, thinking how Ben Davis must have scurried home to tell Janet what had happened. And he hadn't even been out of breath.

When the meal was over, Davis said, "Dusk already. We dawdle any longer an' you won't be able to see nuthin'."

They hurried then along the creek to Davis's wood yard, a little over a quarter of a mile away.

The first thing Cole saw was the wood. Almost exclusively cedar, sawed into four-foot chunks, it was piled nearly twenty feet high in the center of the yard. Cole guessed the pile must have been over a hundred feet in diameter — enough wood to last the town of Cedar through two cold winters.

Davis led him around the pile, aromatic with the peculiar but pleasant smell of cedar, and then Cole saw the rig of which the old man was so proud. And he had cause to be, Cole thought. The old steam tractor was taller than a man. It looked like a railroad locomotive minus the cab and flanged drive wheels. Its stack was five feet high, rising from a boiler almost two feet in diameter. The stack was belled and screened at the top to catch burning cinders before they flew out and set fire to the wood.

The rig was painted bright red. The front wheels were about three feet in diameter, made of iron, and the rear ones over four. Diagonal flanges on the treads were intended to give it traction in soft ground. On the right of the boiler was a large pulley wheel, connected by a belt to the saw mandrel which was mounted at the tractor's rear.

Davis chuckled proudly. "Damn thing'll go ten miles an hour. Sounds like a hundred iron-shod horses on a hard road. She clanks like hell. Even without the whistle, I reckon you can hear her comin' a mile off."

Cole looked around at the rest of the yard. Fenced with poles, it covered more than an acre of ground. At the rear were open-fronted stables, and behind them, fenced separately, was a stack of wild hay. One stable held two big, sleek work teams, munching contentedly at a manger filled with hay.

At the other end of the yard were the cedar logs Davis had skidded down for sawing. When Davis saw Cole looking at them, he said, "You can see why I need a man. Takes two to heft them things. Way I do it now is to set one end up to the saw, t'other on them rails I got set up to hold 'em. But it's slower'n molasses on a cold Christmas mornin'." He grinned. "But why the hell should I worry? I got wood enough sawed to keep us eatin' for two years if I could sell it."

"You'll sell, come winter," Cole said grimly. "By then Keldson's goose is going to be cooked."

Davis cocked his head and looked at Cole. Then he grinned. "I reckon it will. I reckon it will at that."

As he turned, Davis's grin faded, and Cole heard the old man mutter, "If you live, friend. If they don't do you like they done Bud."

Chapter Eleven

Cole was up before dawn to be on Triangle Mesa by the time the sun was up. He went out into the cool morning air and crossed the bridge into town.

No mark in the street where the gunman had lain. He walked to the stable, found and saddled his horse. He rode out without seeing a soul and climbed to the mesa top.

He took up his vigil, but Sidonie did not appear all day.

The next day, Saturday, his patience at an end, he rode boldly in to Chain and asked for the girl. Zelda opened the door only long enough to say, "She's not here, and I wouldn't let you see her if she was." She shut the door in his face and he heard the bolt slam home.

He turned away, thinking that up to now he had found Sidonie wary, even unfriendly. He knew she would have heard the story of the gunman's death. If he talked to her, it must be when no one else was present. If he was to convince her, he must tell her the full story of his friendship with Andy, and of Andy's death.

He considered writing her a letter, asking her to see him, but he discarded the idea immediately, knowing he could not be sure the letter would be delivered to her. Could it be that Sidonie was a prisoner on Chain? He had to admit the possibility.

Riding back to town, he decided to see Judge Benson again. Certainly Benson had the answers or some of them at least. Probably he wasn't ready to talk, but the time must come when he would be.

Cole entered town and saw Dick Walters emerge from a small saddlery shop lugging a weather-beaten saddle to which a bright, new sheepskin lining had been added. Walters squinted at him, then flipped the saddle onto his horse's blanketed back. Turning, he motioned for Cole to stop. Cole halted. Walters cinched down his newly repaired saddle, mounted and rode to midstreet where he sat slumped in his saddle, studying Cole with a touch of reserve in his eyes.

"Looks like I pegged you wrong, Knapp," Walters said finally. "When I met up with you the night we chased the Carew girl, I figured you for another gunslinger Keldson had fetched to the country. I was wrong."

"You were," Cole agreed. "Whether you knew it or not we've been on the same side all along."

"I know that now," Walters admitted. "I found it out the next day when Marty worked you over in the Staghorn. Mind you, I ain't apologizin' for not sidin' you. There was only Herb Pomeroy an' me against the whole Chain crew. We couldn't have helped you."

Cole realized this was true. He asked, grinning faintly, "You didn't think you'd get Rhodes to let me go by coming to the jail, did you?"

"No, but I figured he'd tell Benson it wasn't your fault. Guess if he did, it didn't help none. But how come Miss Carew bailed you out?"

"She hoped I'd leave the country."

"Goin' to?"

"No."

This seemed to encourage Walters. Cole studied him, realizing that his first judgment of the man had been too harsh. Walters was trying to fill Bud Davis's shoes, and he wasn't enough man to do it. Still, he was willing to try.

"If Benson ever brings you to trial,"

Walters said, "you got two witnesses on your side. Me'n Herb'll tell what really happened."

Cole saw what this promise cost Walters, and said, "Never mind. It's not going to amount to anything more'n a fine. No use getting Keldson down on you for that."

Walters put a hand on his saddle horn. His gaze rested thoughtfully on the Chain house on the mesa. He said slowly, "Comes a time when a man looks real close at himself in his shavin' mirror. If he don't like what he sees, he'd better change it. Herb an' me'll testify. It ain't a big thing, but if enough of us fight that damned Keldson in little ways —"

Cole held out his hand and Walters took it, gripping hard. Cole asked, "Is Keldson any different from old Bill Carew?"

"Plenty. Bill was tough, but he had a stoppin' place. Keldson ain't got any. That's why the rest of us are so scared. We ain't sold out to him yet, but reckon we will. Ain't no other way, as long as Keldson's alive."

"Don't sell yet," Cole said quickly. "Maybe you won't have to. But I need more time."

"How much time? We all got letters from Keldson saying we had a week to take his offers for our ranches. Dunno what his

129

scheme is, but he's got something up his sleeve."

Silence ribboned out for a full minute, with Walters staring toward the monstrous stone house on the mesa. His expression was bitter, as though he had reached the end of his string.

"Anything else on your mind, Walters?" Cole asked.

"Nothin' else," Walters mumbled. But then he straightened and his gaze lay steadily on Cole's face. "Yes, there was somethin' else." He swallowed with difficulty, then went on, "I know what I am, and I ain't overly proud of it. Bud Davis's pa says we're just a bunch of talk'n spit men, an' he's sure right. When Bud was alive and headed up the Regulators we leaned on him. Maybe we would have followed him if it came to a fight. But right now we ain't goin' nowhere. Can't agree on nothin'. What I really stopped you for was to ask if you'd take Bud's place. You ain't afraid of Keldson. I seen that the day he beat you up."

"I came here to do a job," Cole said. "I won't leave till it's done. I can use your help as much as you can use mine."

Walters was silent a moment, his eyes fixed on Cole. Finally he said, "We're havin' a meetin' at my place Monday night. You be

130

there. By that time we'll know what Keldson's schemin' to do."

He nodded and rode past Cole. Hipping around in his saddle, Cole stared at the man's back. He couldn't in honesty criticize Walters. The man was middle-aged and had a family. All he wanted was the right to live in peace and work for his family. Keldson was denying him even that right.

Cole rode on, wondering what Keldson had up his sleeve that made him think he could force Walters and the others to decide in a week. And if they did agree to sell, would he buy their ranches? Cole was sure Sidonie would have no part of a game like this, a plain squeeze-out.

Perhaps Sidonie didn't know what was happening. She seldom came to town or saw her neighbors. Maybe she knew no more of what was going on than Keldson and his mother wanted her to know. Still, she was Bill Carew's daughter, and there must be some of his toughness in her. Sooner or later she'd find out what was going on and would defy Keldson.

Cole left his horse at the livery stable, finding Dusty Rhodes sullenly hostile. He hadn't spoken a dozen words to Cole since he'd been proved wrong the evening of the gunfight. The gunman with the fast gun was dead and Cole was alive. Rhodes apparently found that hard to believe.

He took the reins from Cole, saying with grudging admiration, "Found out the name of that gunslinger you shot. Dakota Ed Sanders. Had a big reputation up north."

"Man can make a reputation any of a dozen ways," Cole said.

"Next time it'll be Duke Le Clair," Rhodes blurted. "You ain't gonna find him so easy —" He halted abruptly, realizing what he'd said.

Cole grinned, but there was an edge to his voice. "Don't worry, Dusty. You didn't tell me anything I didn't already know, or suspect." Suddenly angered, he seized the deputy's arm. "Mister, you've pussyfooted around doing Chain's chores long enough. If it wasn't for yahoos like you and the judge, this country wouldn't be in the shape it's in. Let me tell you something. Keldson's goin' to die. The day he does, you'd better be damned hard to find."

Rhodes jerked free and led the horse toward his stall. Cole left the stable, aware of the futility of putting pressure on Rhodes. The man was a rabbit.

At supper that night Cole told Janet and Ben Davis about his meeting with Dick Walters. Davis nodded, smiling with pride as Cole told him what Walters had said about Bud. "He was a fighting man, by grab." Then the little man frowned. "Why'd Keldson give 'em a week? What can he do in a week? Less'n he's goin' to raid 'em."

Cole shrugged. "What makes you think he won't raid?" Janet asked. "Human life means nothing to him."

Davis didn't answer. He was studying Cole. He said, "You've brought this thing to a head. You're the cocklebur under Keldson's saddle. You watch your step. Maybe you're the key. Maybe he's allowin' a week to dry-gulch you, knowin' if he gets you the Regulators will fold. He damned near had 'em when you showed up."

Janet was looking at Cole, apparently wanting to say something and not quite sure she should. He finished his pie and leaned back in his chair. He grinned at her. "Say it, lady. What's on your mind?"

She gave him a shaky smile. "I want you to stay alive. I'm afraid for you. You're so like Bud. And Bud's dead."

Cole's smile faded. "What's she driving at, Ben?"

Davis said cryptically, "This is Satiddy night." He shoved his chair back and stood up. "No use talkin' to him, Janet. He won't listen."

She rose and started clearing the table. Faintly irritated, Cole said, "Stop beating around the bush. What are you trying to say?"

"You're bullheaded," Janet said. "That's what I'm trying to say. Bud was bullheaded, too, and the more we pleaded with him, the more bullheaded he got."

Suddenly Cole knew what was in their minds. This was Saturday night and the whole Chain crew would be in town. They were trying to tell him he should stay inside, like a rabbit hiding in his hole.

"Thanks for worrying about me," he said gently, "but I had no intention of hunting for trouble in the Staghorn. Anyway, the pressure's on Keldson."

He got up and went out through the door. Davis was on the front porch, his rocking chair making a steady, squeaking sound. Cole sat down and leaned against a post, enjoying the moment of evening quiet.

Dusk became night but the heat of the day still lingered. For a time there was no sound except the chirping of a cricket under the porch and the liquid whisper of the creek lapping against the willows. For that moment even Davis's chair was silent.

The stillness was blasted suddenly by the rumble of hoofs on the hard-packed dirt of

Main Street and a volley of gunfire. Davis sighed. "There they are. It's the same every Satiddy night except durin' roundup or when they're drivin' to the railroad."

Cole put his head back against the post and closed his eyes. He thought how much different this country would be if Bill Carew had never married Zelda and brought her to Chain. Marty wouldn't be here, but Andy would. Andy would be ramrodding Chain and there would be no trouble. Andy would have been satisfied with what he had.

The sound of footsteps brought Cole upright, his hand grabbing for the gun at his side. Davis said, "Easy, son. I've had my eyes open. It's only the Ronson kid."

A boy appeared out of the darkness to stand in the shaft of lamplight that fell through the open doorway. He said hesitantly, "I'm lookin' for Mr. Knapp."

Cole had seen the boy around town. He said, "You've found him."

The boy backed a step, his gaze fastening itself on Cole with awe. He said, "Mr. Keldson gave me four bits to tell you he wanted to see you. He's yonder at the bridge — alone. Said to tell you he just wants to talk."

The boy whirled and ran, and the sound of his steps died in the direction of the bridge. Davis leaned forward, laying a hand on Cole's shoulder. "Don't go. It's a trap." He paused, then he said, "That was wasted breath, wasn't it?"

Cole nodded.

Davis said, "Damn it, chances are there's a dozen of 'em there. They'll cut you down."

"Not in the dark. I told you Keldson's feeling the pressure. I'm going to find out just how jumpy he is."

He got up and loosened his gun in the holster. He walked toward the bridge. Halfway there, he slowed and angled toward the creek.

In the damp grass along the bank his feet were silent. He moved slowly and carefully until he made out Keldson's bulky shape beside the bridge. He waited a full minute, probing the darkness with his eyes. Satisfied that Keldson was alone, he said, "I'm here, Keldson."

Keldson jumped. "You damn Injun! I didn't hear you."

"Didn't aim for you to. What's on your mind?"

"Talk. You got me wrong, Knapp. It's time I was setting you right."

"Like you did in the Staghorn, maybe?"

"That was a mistake. I figured you were a gunslick the Regulators hired to get me.

Now I know I was wrong. A hired gun wouldn't have hung around after taking the beating you got."

Cole smiled in the darkness. This was a twist. Walters had figured Cole was a gunman imported by Chain. He said, "So?"

"Just wanted you to know how it is with Chain. We're fighting for our life. Everybody's against us because we're big. Hell, it ain't a crime to be big, Knapp, but I say folks are against us. That's why we've got to keep on getting bigger. They'll chew us up if we don't."

Cole waited, silent.

Keldson said, "I'm going to hold Chain together and I don't care what it costs. I ain't giving up a blade of grass to nobody."

Cole said warily, "Go on."

"I make it a point to know where every man in the country stands. I want to know where you stand and what you're doing here."

"My business. Anything else?"

"I'm looking out for Sidonie's interests. If you're here to hurt her —"

"I'm not."

Keldson was silent, and it seemed to Cole he could feel the anger growing in the big man. Keldson demanded, "Then why are you here?"

137

"Worry about that, Keldson."

For a moment Keldson stood there, his breathing a rasping sound that was audible even above the rush of water in the stream beneath the bridge. Suddenly he turned and strode away, his boots hammering on the plank floor of the bridge. Turning his head, Cole saw Ben Davis a few feet behind him, almost hidden by the willows. Starshine glinted briefly on the barrel of a shotgun Davis held.

"What the hell, Ben?"

Davis laid a hand on his arm. "Wait," he whispered. "Watch over yonder."

They waited, and presently three men appeared from the willows on the other side of the bridge. They took the street toward town. Davis said, "I told you it was a trap. Had you come walkin' along past where they was, they'd have sprung it."

Walking back, Davis said, "I heard most of the talk. You know something, boy. And Keldson knows you know. He'll never let you go."

"You've got that wrong, Ben," Cole said. "I'll never let him go."

Chapter Twelve

Some time after midnight, Ben Davis shook Cole by the shoulder. "Janet's time's come," he whispered hoarsely. "She's two weeks early, but it's come."

Cole fumbled on the stand beside the bed, found a match and thumbed it into life. He lighted the lamp, sat up, and yawned. Suddenly the significance of what Davis had said got through his sleep-fogged mind. He said irritably, "What do you expect me to do?" He was scared at the prospect of childbirth, and wondered now why he had come here in the first place. This reality he had never expected to face. He had assumed he'd be gone long before Janet had her baby.

"I don't know," Davis said helplessly. "But I don't know what to do, neither. She's in a lot of pain — comes and goes. When it comes, she moans and groans, and that ain't like her, so it must be bad."

Cole was fully awake now. He realized

suddenly how helpless Ben Davis felt, and that shocked him, for Davis was a fierce little terrier who had always impressed Cole as being able to handle anything. Tonight that fierceness was stripped from him. He stood in the doorway staring down at Cole, turning to him because Cole was the only one he could trust to help.

Cole pulled on his pants, asking, "How much time have we got?" He realized his hands were shaking, something they never did.

"I dunno," Davis answered. "Hell, I never had no babies. I mean, we had Bud, but I wasn't even home when he came."

"We'll get somebody," Cole said. "I'll fetch the doc. Janet'll have to have a woman, too. You tell me who to get and I'll get her."

"Doc'll be drunk," Davis said, "and there ain't a woman in town who'd come. But I ain't worried 'bout that. Janet's strong. She'll be up an' around, takin' care of the baby afore you know it. It's — it's right now that's got me buffaloed."

Cole pulled on his boots and stood up. "Ben, don't tell me we can't get a woman to come here in a case like this. It's got nothing to do with Marty Keldson or Chain."

"Yes, it has," the little man said. "I tell you he's passed the word. Nobody'll have nothin' to do with us. It's just like my wood yard. I've got stuff piled to hell-and-gone, but nobody'll buy a stick of it."

Cole buckled on his gun. "Make some coffee. Strong and black. I'll get Doc here if I have to drag him." He picked up his hat and started toward the door, calling back as he went through it, "Doc'll need hot water. I know that much about babies coming. Get a fire going and put a boiler of water on the stove."

He left the house at a run, crossed the bridge and climbed the stairs to Holt's office over the bank. If the doctor was in, Cole knew he could handle him. The problem would be different if Doc was out of town.

Women had borne children and taken care of themselves. They'd lived through it, too, but it shouldn't happen to Janet. It was bad enough that her husband wouldn't be with her when she bore her child. To be uncared for was just too much. Mentally Cole marked another score against Marty Keldson.

The door of the doctor's office was open, and lamplight fell through it into the hall. Cole breathed a sigh of relief. Doc was up and awake, so maybe it wouldn't be too bad. But when Cole stepped through the doorway and looked at the doctor, he knew he was wrong. Holt was on his feet beside his desk, a whisky bottle in his hand. He was tired; his clothes were dirty. He stared at Cole blearily as though he had never seen him before.

Cole said harshly, "Get your bag, Doc. Janet Davis is having her baby."

"I'm not going anywhere," Doc said thickly. "I just got back from Stony Crest. A rock fell on a man and busted him all to hell. I'm beat. I'm going to bed."

"Not now, Doc." Cole picked up the black bag from the desk and grabbed Holt by the shoulder. "You're going to deliver Janet's baby. Come on."

Stubbornness took hold of the doctor, stubbornness and the liquor he had consumed on the way back from Stony Crest. He pulled away, slapping at Cole peevishly. "Lemme alone! I'll see her tomorrow. Women can have babies just like cattle if they're as healthy as Janet is. Nothin'll stop 'em once they start."

Cole slapped him sharply on the side of the face. "Damn you, Doc. You're coming if I have to drag you."

Holt backed up a step. "I dunno who you think you are, but you can't —"

Patience gone, Cole grabbed Holt by an

arm and pulled him bodily to the door. Holt tried to hold back. Then the resistance went out of him and he began to sob with maudlin self-pity, "You can't do this to me. A man's got some dignity —"

"You haven't," Cole said disgustedly. He had Doc on the landing now. Maybe the cool night air — "Come on," he said. "Stay on your feet. If I throw you downstairs, you'll break your damned neck."

Still Holt held back. Exasperated, Cole put an arm around his ample waist and tried to drag him down the stairs. "Get ahold of that railing. Start walking, damn you."

Holt obeyed until he was halfway down, then he stopped. He said with drunken cunning, "You can't make me go. I won't be no good to nobody if I break my neck."

Cole released his hold around the doctor's waist, pulled his hand free from the railing and pushed him down the stairs. Holt fell like a sack of wool, thumping on the stairs as he rolled over and over until he hit the ground. He was too drunk to be hurt. He could have fallen off Triangle Mesa, Cole thought, and got up and walked away. When Cole reached the bottom, Holt was already sitting up.

"You pushed me," Holt accused. "You let me fall."

Cole pulled him to his feet. "Walk then, damn it, or I'll pitch you into the creek. Then you'll sober up or drown."

Holt walked, lurching from side to side. Cole's right hand steadied him with a firm grip on his coat collar. He fell twice, and both times Cole yanked him to his feet and pushed him on. By the time they reached the Davis house, Holt was moving more steadily and under his own power.

"Pour the coffee, Ben," Cole said.

Even with the door to Janet's room shut, he could hear her. She did not scream, but every now and then the pain would wrench a groan or a sharp moan from her. The sounds both frightened and angered Cole because he couldn't help thinking of Marty Keldson, and of Bud Davis who would be with Janet now if he hadn't been murdered.

Davis handed him a cup of steaming coffee, staring at Holt. "He's filthy, Cole. He ain't worth a damn. Kick him out."

Cole took the cup and grabbing a handful of the doctor's hair, shook his head savagely. "Drink, Doc. Get this down, you hear?" He put the cup to Holt's lips and tipped it. Some of the scalding coffee went down his throat, the rest down both sides of his mouth. Cole handed the empty cup to Davis. "Fill it up again. I'll get it down him

144

or choke him to death."

The second cup went down better than the first. Then Cole pumped a bucket of water and bringing it to Holt, shoved his head into it. He brought Holt's head out just long enough for the strangling man to take a breath, then shoved it in again. He pulled Holt's head out a second time and then poured the water into the sink.

Holt was sputtering and gasping, but his eyes were clearer now. Cole said, "Get a pan of warm water and some soap. He'll be all right once we clean him up."

Davis brought the water and soap. Cole got a towel. He watched the doctor, knowing exactly how he felt, but without sympathy.

Holt stripped off his coat and rolled up his sleeves. He gripped the side of the table a moment, then began to wash.

He was thorough. Cole gave him credit for that. When he was through, he dried himself and turned, something of authority in his eyes for the first time. He said, "Keep the fire going. I need plenty of hot water. I'll take a look at her now. Fetch me some white cloths, Ben, a lot of them."

Holt picked up his black bag and went into Janet's bedroom. Cole told himself there was nothing more he could do. He couldn't stay here and listen to Janet. He went out of the house, lit a lantern and spent an hour splitting wood. He brought an armload into the kitchen and filled the firebox in the big range and went out again.

He walked to the bridge and sat down, staring at the water below him. It glittered in the middle of the stream like obsidian where the starshine touched it. He smoked one cigarette after another, thinking first of Andy Carew, then of Sidonie, and finally, with hatred, of Marty Keldson.

Then, because he could stand idleness no longer, he went back to the house. Davis was pacing the kitchen floor. He shook his head at Cole when he saw him. "Nothin's happened yet. Nothin' we can do, either, Doc says. Just wait. Janet's sufferin'. Damn it, if there was just somethin' we could do! If Bud was only here —"

"She's got to have a woman," Cole said. "Who'll I get?"

"Nobody. I told you nobody'd come."

"I'll get Benson's wife. She's your neighbor."

"That old biddy wouldn't come. No use askin'."

"I'll get her," Cole said, and left the house.

The Benson house was on the same side

of the creek as the Davis place, and was a two-story brick structure that had at one time made claim to elegance. Now, like most of Cedar, it had lost its dignity through sheer neglect.

Dawn was beginning to show above the mountains far to the east when Cole jerked the bell pull. He waited a few seconds, then yanked again, then a third time angrily. At last he saw a light and heard someone moving inside the house.

Another minute passed before the door opened. Judge Benson stood there with a lamp in his hand. He wore a dark purple dressing-gown and leather slippers, and somehow he contrived to maintain his dignity in spite of the hour and his attire. The instant he identified his visitor his face turned dark with anger. He would have slammed the door in Cole's face if Cole had not put a foot across the threshold and bulled his way in, forcing Benson back.

"Don't get high and mighty with me now, Judge," Cole said, "or I'll skin the hide right off your back."

Benson set the lamp on the table. "What do you want? Say it and get out of my house."

"I want your wife. Janet Davis is having her baby and she needs a woman to take care of her."

"Damn you, do you think my wife would —"

"She'd better, Judge. She'd just better."

Benson squared his shoulders. "My wife is not at the beck and call of any —"

"Don't say it, Judge." Cole's voice was dangerously soft. Then he walked to Benson and looked him straight in the eyes. "Judge, isn't there any decency left in Cedar? Isn't there anyone who feels like a human being? Or has all your humanity run down a gopher hole because you're scared of what Marty Keldson might do?"

Benson didn't answer. His lips moved, but no words came. Cole said, "I've listened to Janet tonight, Judge. She's suffering. She needs help and she's going to get it. Way I look at it, it's as much your fault her husband's dead as it is Keldson's. Yours and Dusty Rhodes and everybody else's in this stinking, yellow town. Now go get your wife before I lose my temper."

The Judge turned and disappeared into the rear of the house. He returned a few moments later with his wife — a tall, angular woman who did not so much as nod a greeting to Cole. She went out through the door into the pale dawn light with Cole following. Reaching the Davis house, she entered and went at once into Janet's bedroom.

Ben Davis was sitting in a chair, grinning like a little boy. He looked up at Cole, still grinning, but with a kind of wonder in his eyes. "It's a boy, Cole, the dangedest little ole red-faced mite you ever seen. Got all his toes an' fingers, too."

Cole grinned back at the little man. "That's fine, Ben. Real fine."

Davis looked at him, his face turning grave. "Cole, I ain't much for words, but mebbe you know how I feel. Thanks. I dunno what we'd of done tonight if it wasn't for you."

"Forget it. You hear?" Cole swallowed and sat down. "What's Janet naming the boy?"

"Benjamin Harrison Davis Three."

"Why the Three?"

"That's plain enough. I'm Benjamin Harrison Davis One, an' Bud, he was Benjamin Harrison Davis Two. The boy's just gotta be Three, don't he?"

Cole chuckled. "I guess he does, Ben. I guess he does at that."

Chapter Thirteen

Sidonie Carew was aware that Cole had been on Chain range. Or at least she knew someone had been watching the house. She had found two different spots, both in view of the Chain buildings, where cigarette stubs littered the ground and testified to it.

Riding out this morning, she stopped at one of the places where she had found the cigarette stubs. She dismounted and sat down with her back to a cedar where Cole must have sat. What had he thought about, sitting here? Chain and whatever scheme he had for making a profit for himself? Marty and Zelda had said repeatedly that was why Cole was here, and sometimes she almost believed it.

Or had Cole thought about Sidonie herself? Or of the man he had killed? Had he thought of that man's sister?

She got up, impatient with herself and angry because her thoughts strayed so often to Cole and without any volition on her part. He meant nothing to her. He was a trouble-maker, a killer who probably had never held a job more than three months running. He was quarrelsome. By his own admission he had come here to make trouble.

Sidonie got up restlessly and mounted; but her thoughts did not leave Cole nor did her irritation with herself depart.

The truth was she wanted to see Cole again. She knew he had killed. She suspected he had done worse, and would do worse before he left the country. But she couldn't forget him. He had made too strong an impression on her.

Sidonie had not had many suitors, and none of those few had been around long enough to become serious. Zelda had seen to that, making it uncomfortable for them and telling her they were not worthy of her. Or they were afraid of Marty, and they had reason to be.

That brought her thoughts again to Cole. *He was the only man she had ever met who was not afraid of Marty.*

Irritated by her own confusion, Sidonie rode back to the house, though it was only mid-morning. She went inside and would have gone to her room if Zelda had not called to her from the parlor.

Sidonie went in and sank wearily into a chair, confused and wishing there was someone she trusted in whom she could confide. She felt disloyal, realizing she was beginning to distrust Zelda.

"When are you and Marty going to get married, dear?" Zelda asked.

Sidonie almost blurted, "We're not." But she didn't. Instead she said, "I don't know. Not until this trouble is settled at least."

"You can't keep him dangling. He's a man and he's impatient. If he had you to keep him occupied, he'd be less — Well, he'd be more content just to run the ranch."

Sidonie almost laughed. What Zelda really meant was that Marty would be less quarrelsome. But she didn't laugh. This was too serious for that. She had known for a long time that Zelda wanted her to marry Marty. She had never committed herself one way or the other, and now she realized it was something she could not put off indefinitely. She might just as well have an understanding now.

She said, "I don't love him. I won't marry a man I don't love."

Sidonie caught a glimpse of something like hardened steel in her stepmother, a quality that was usually hidden behind the façade of gentleness with which Zelda usually treated her.

Color rushed into Zelda's face and anger touched her mouth. "If it wasn't for the ranch —"

Suddenly Sidonie was angry, too. "What do you mean?"

"Nothing. I'm sorry."

"Don't be sorry. I want the truth. Do you mean that if it wasn't for the ranch, Marty wouldn't want to marry me?"

"Of course not," Zelda said, her composure returning. "I meant that if it wasn't for the ranch, there'd be no hurry about your marrying Marty. But Chain's in trouble, whether you know it or not. The way it is, Marty's risking his life for property that belongs to you. But if you were married, it would be his, too. His and yours." She paused. "You need a strong hand, dear. Marty wants to be that strong hand."

"I don't need his help. There'd be less trouble if Marty's hands weren't always beating someone up, always threatening, always bullying."

"Sidonie!"

"It's true, no matter what you think Marty is. He's a bully and he's greedy. Making Chain the biggest ranch in Colorado may be important to Marty, but it's not to me. Not when it means killing men and beating them and intimidating everyone who stands in the way."

"What are you trying to say?" There was an odd tone in Zelda's voice.

"Nothing, except what I said. And I meant every word." Sidonie stood up.

Zelda's voice was still quiet when she said, "Stubbornness, my dear, is one thing neither Marty nor I will stand. You will marry him, you know. Bud Davis found out what stubbornness does to Marty. So did Cole Knapp. The others will find out in a few days, too, as soon as Marty gets done at Stony Crest —"

She halted abruptly, as though realizing she had said too much. She softened immediately and touched Sidonie's arm with her hand. "Let's not quarrel, dear. Your father's gone and Andy will never come back. We don't have anyone but each other. And Marty."

Sidonie stood staring at her stepmother. Stony Crest, as she knew, was the name given an outcropping of rock at the northeast corner of Triangle Mesa. It lay between Coroner Creek and Big Horse Creek. At this point the two streams ran less than a hundred yards apart before they separated again to flow on both sides of Triangle

Mesa. Big Horse ran through the meadows of the Regulators and the town of Cedar. Coroner Creek watered Chain's hay meadows on the other side of the mesa.

"What did you mean about Stony Crest?" Sidonie asked.

Zelda, unreasonably agitated, rose from her chair. Sidonie repeated, sharply this time, "What did you mean about Stony Crest?"

"Nothing. Nothing at all." Abruptly, Zelda turned and went upstairs.

Sidonie watched her go. Then, deeply troubled by what Zelda had said and by her question that had gone unanswered, she left the house and crossed the yard to the barn. Her mare was still in her stall, munching the oats she had given her. She bridled and saddled quickly and rode out. As she left, she noticed Zelda watching from an upstairs window. When she was almost out of earshot, Sidonie heard a call from the house behind her. She turned to see if it was for her but she could not distinguish the words. Apparently it was Zelda shouting for the choreman.

That remark about Stony Crest — What was it Zelda had said? *When Marty gets done at Stony Crest* —

She lifted the mare into an easy canter,

and rode northeast toward the point of rock that was called Stony Crest. The ridge which seemed to terminate beyond the end of Triangle Mesa was actually a continuation of the mesa. The two were connected by a low saddle.

Sidonie's first awareness that she was being followed came when she heard the hoofs of a running horse behind her. She turned her head to see Cole riding toward her. Apparently he had been coming from town to resume his scrutiny of the house and had seen her riding away.

"Hey, wait a minute," he yelled, and somewhat reluctantly she reined in to wait. She did not particularly want to talk to him. Yet in spite of all she had been told, in spite of the things she knew he had done, she realized all at once that she had nothing to fear from Cole Knapp.

He pulled up, took off his hat and smiled at her. He said, "I've been wanting to talk to you."

"I know. I've seen a couple of the places where you waited. You smoke too much, Mr. Knapp."

He grinned. "Probably. But that's not what I wanted to talk to you about."

Suddenly she blamed him for her own confusion and unhappiness. She asked, deliberately wanting to hurt him, "What did you want to talk about — the man you killed in Cedar?"

His face turned grave. "So you've heard?"

"Who hasn't? You're becoming famous, you know — as a killer."

She saw that hurt, and she was immediately ashamed of having said it and of her desire to hurt him.

"Please listen to me," he said. "I never saw that man before in my life, or his sister either, if he had one. He was hired to kill me." She was silent. Then he asked, "You don't believe me, do you?"

"I don't know what to believe."

He dismounted and stood looking at her. His voice was soft, gentle, and sympathetic. "I wanted to talk to you about your brother. Andy was my friend — my very close friend."

She was not surprised. She looked down at his strong, dark face, not the face of a gentle man, but still a face that she found attractive. Could a man like this look her straight in the eye and lie? She managed to say, "Go on."

"I tried to tell you before, the day you got me out of jail. This time I hope you'll listen. He's dead. I want to tell you about it."

She slid off her horse. "I'll listen."

"I think you're in danger, just like Andy was and for the same reason. Chain is a big stake, Sidonie, and Marty Keldson wants it. Marty knows Andy's dead. Marty had him killed. If you were dead, too, or if you were married to Marty, Chain would be his." He paused, his face very grave. "I doubt that you'd marry a man like Marty Keldson. Do you see what his other alternative is?"

She felt her heart pound. What he had said tied in so sharply with what she had just seen in Zelda, a new and frightening Zelda, who had threatened, reminding her of what had happened to Bud Davis.

"I don't think you realize what kind of man Keldson is," Cole hurried on, "even though you've grown up with him. Janet's had her baby, but there wasn't a woman who would come to her house and look after her. I finally got Mrs. Benson, but I thought for a while I'd have to break the Judge's neck to get her to come. Ben said there wasn't any use to ask her. Or anybody else. He keeps saying Keldson's passed the word."

She was sick with the thought that because of Marty's cruelty the women of Cedar were afraid to help Janet Davis, Janet who had lost her husband because of Marty's vicious greed. *But she was the key to that greed.* If she married him, or if she died,

Chain would go to Zelda, and in the end, to Marty.

From the direction of Chain came the hammering beat of a horse's hoofs. "Keldson," Cole said, and swore under his breath. "Mount up, Sidonie. This will be something you won't want to watch."

Keldson slid his horse to a halt and hit the ground running. His eyes were ugly. "So this is why you won't marry me. You've been meeting Knapp out here in the brush all the time."

"Marty!"

He looked at her sullenly. "You stay the hell out of this."

"I won't stay out of this, and I won't be spoken to like that."

He laughed, a nasty, grating sound. "Now ain't you the high and mighty one? Listen, girl. I'm going to beat this drifter so he can't walk."

He had always shown her some deference, some courtesy, but now she saw only rage and hate. He looked at her as if he despised her. "You think you can beat him without having your men hold him?" she said. "You don't need to try. You're through at Chain. I want you and Zelda out of the house by sundown. I'll have your things sent wherever you want."

For an instant Marty looked as if he didn't understand what she'd said. Then he threw back his head and laughed.

Cole touched her arm. "Go home. This is between us." His eyes were angry, his mouth grim, but she felt a gentleness in him. And suddenly she trusted him.

She climbed to her saddle and turned her horse toward Chain. She did not look back. But before she had gone a hundred yards she heard the sounds of their coming together behind her.

Chapter Fourteen

For an instant the heads of both men were turned, watching the girl ride away. Then, from the corner of his eye, Cole caught Keldson's movement. He swung his head warily.

Keldson was watching him, eyes narrowed and filled with the same sadistic pleasure Cole had seen in them the day Keldson had beaten him in the Staghorn saloon.

The memory of that day drove all caution out of Cole. Here was his enemy, and now was his time. There would be no one today to hold his arms. Keldson would fight, and he would bear the marks of his fighting for the rest of his life.

As they stared at each other, both men seemed to have forgotten their guns. Suddenly Cole charged and closed with Keldson. He feinted with his right, and when Keldson came in to follow up, smashed him solidly in the mouth with a hard left hand.

Keldson's head snapped back, and now Cole laid his right on with all the power of his shoulders behind it. It spread Keldson's nose like a ripe grape, and left it broken and bloody.

Keldson answered with his great fists, and now Cole made no effort to avoid them, concentrating instead on seeing that every blow he threw at Keldson landed and punished the man.

They fought like primeval men, without science or skill. They simply stood spraddle-legged and traded punch for punch, until the sounds of their fists landing had a sodden, sickening sound similar to that of a cleaver slicing through flesh and bone on a butcher's meat block.

Neither noticed that Sidonie had stopped a quarter of a mile away to watch. Neither saw her turn her face away.

Cole relished each shock of pain that passed along his arm as the bones of his hands met the bone of Keldson's face. He shook his head whenever one of Keldson's fists stunned him, but still he bore in.

His right laid Keldson's cheek open. His left brought a swelling bruise the size of a plum to Keldson's forehead. He broke Keldson's teeth, and Keldson spat them out on the ground. He punished the man's ribs until each succeeding blow brought a sharp intake of painful breath to Keldson's lungs.

He did not escape the punishment of Keldson's blows. But today he was able to roll with many of them, and so avoid much of the destructiveness of their brutal force.

His face became battered and bled on his shirt. His belly and ribs and chest showed bright red through his torn shirt where Keldson's fists had stung them.

On and on it went, until Sidonie, out on the mesa, could stand no more. She turned her horse and rode toward Chain to get men who could stop the fight before both fighters were dead.

Keldson tired at last, and so did Cole, though neither seemed to realize it. Yet their tiredness showed in the slowing of their straining bodies. It showed in the lessening of the force behind each blow.

Keldson's eyes glazed, but the hatred in them kept them alive. Cole's arms became as lead until it was all he could do to lift them and throw them forward.

Keldson fell, and Cole staggered and fell himself before he could reach his enemy. They fought on their knees, still trading blows. Cole knocked Keldson down and sprawled across the man. He struggled to his knees again to find that Keldson had also struggled up.

Angered at his own tiredness, his own ineffectiveness, Cole put forth a mighty surge and got to his feet. For an instant he stood looking down at Keldson who had neither the strength nor the will to imitate him.

Then Cole moved in for the kill, feeling no compassion for Keldson, feeling nothing but the overpowering need to destroy. He stood two feet from Keldson, breathing hard, waiting for strength to return to his leaden arms.

He could wait no more. He drew his right back, lifted his shoulder and drove his whole body forward to give impetus to the driving, bloody fist.

If Keldson had ducked or swayed aside, Cole would have missed, and sprawled headlong on the ground. But Keldson could not move. He stayed on his knees, eyes glazed with pain.

Cole's fist took him squarely between the eyes, and they fell together in a heap on the ground.

It was fully a minute before Cole could move. Then he stirred, groaned, and again struggled to his feet.

Head hanging with weariness, chest heaving, he stared down at his unconscious foe. Keldson lay on his back, mouth sagging open, broken teeth showing and exposed to the air. His breathing was scarcely visible.

Cole wondered if the man would die, and hoped he would. He stared down and at last found words. "That was for Andy and Bud Davis. It was for me, too, for the day in the Staghorn."

He could not have said how long it took to find his horse. He knew it took considerable doing before he was in the saddle. He started back toward Chain and the road off Triangle Mesa, but he had not gone far when he saw a cloud of dust. Made by nearly a dozen riders, it raised a warning that registered immediately in Cole's mind. Instantly he reined into a gully where he waited until they thundered by.

Danger seemed to have cleared his head, seemed to have given his battered body renewed strength. He gouged his horse's sides and clung to the saddle as the horse moved on again.

Cole knew that if the Chain riders found him today, he was dead. Nothing, not Sidonie, not Ben Davis, not the Regulators, could save him.

So he ran now like a hunted beast. And he was lucky, because he reached the road that led off the mesa before he heard the returning hoofbeats behind him.

Though Cole did not know it, two of them went back to Chain for a buckboard. The others stayed with Keldson, wondering at the man who had done this, wondering, too, if Keldson would live.

Cole stopped at the bridge and fell from his saddle. He crawled to the creek and plunged his face and upper body into the cool water. Revived, he got to his feet, but he did not expend the energy necessary to mount. Instead, he walked until he came to the Davis house.

Ben must have seen him coming, for he ran out and took the reins of Cole's horse. Cole staggered onto the porch and went on through the door. He started across the parlor toward his room, then stopped. Sidonie stood in the kitchen doorway.

Cole tried to grin. He said gently, "I didn't lose. Not this time."

Ben came in through the back. Sidonie said, "There's coffee," and Ben, behind her, said, "Laced with whisky. It's what you need, Cole."

He stumbled into the kitchen and collapsed into a chair. He noticed the way Ben Davis was watching him, and he said, "You oughtta see the other fellow, Ben."

Ben grinned at last. His hands trembled

as he poured whisky into the cup Sidonie had filled with coffee.

"What about Marty?" Sidonie asked. "Did you kill him?"

"No."

Cole held the cup in both hands and sipped it through his battered lips. When he finished, when his stomach was warmed, he looked at Sidonie. "What are you doing here?"

"I've left Chain."

"Why?"

Anger touched her briefly. "Because I will no longer lend my name and my father's name to the things Marty Keldson is doing. Chain's a ranch, not a greedy, warring kingdom. I won't go back as long as Marty and Zelda are there and right now I don't know how to get them off."

Tired as he was, Cole grinned. He looked at Davis. "What do you know about that, Ben?"

But Davis was frankly hostile. "Don't like it," he growled. "Don't like it worth a damn. It's another of Keldson's sneaky tricks."

Cole glanced at Sidonie. No anger showed in her face because of Davis's lack of trust. She said wearily, "I can't blame you for not trusting me, but the trouble you've had is Chain's fault. I just thought I could

167

help until Janet is on her feet again."

"Sounds like a good idea to me, Ben," Cole said. "She'll be a sight more cheerful to look at than Benson's sour-faced wife."

Davis snorted, but he said, "Mebbe, mebbeso."

Cole looked at Sidonie. "You stay. He's grumpy, but his heart's pure gold." He grinned at the way Davis's face flushed at that.

Sidonie said, "It's the least I can do. I'm almost sure Marty killed your son, Mr. Davis."

"Knew it all the time. So did everybody else, I reckon, but you."

"I've been blind, but I'm seeing a few things now."

Cole got up, holding to the back of the chair. He said, "You two fight it out. I'm going to bed."

He staggered across the parlor to his room. He closed the door behind him, then fell, full length, across the bed.

For a few moments his mind was busy. Then he thought that Keldson would not be a threat for a while, a day at least.

Relaxed, he fell into a sleep that was very like unconsciousness.

Chapter Fifteen

Sidonie let Cole sleep as long as possible before knocking on his door and telling him
supper was ready. After he'd eaten, Janet
called him into her room, surprisingly strong
of voice. Her color was good; her eyes were
bright. She was, he saw, a very happy girl.

She looked at his bruised face, sobering.
"Keldson caught you again."

Cole grinned. "Not exactly. You might say
I caught him when there wasn't a bunch of
Chain's riders to hold me for him."

She matched his grin. "What kind of
shape did you leave him in?"

"He wasn't moving. I was. As far as looks
go, we're about the same, I guess."

She sighed and looked proudly at the
baby beside her. She spoke to him softly,
and her voice was troubled. "Not a very nice
world I've brought you into, is it, little
Bud?"

Cole said gently, "By the time he can understand what you're saying, it'll be a pretty good world for him, Janet."

"Do you really believe that?"

"Of course I believe it. There's a Marty Keldson in every community I've ever seen. Some last longer than others, but none of them last forever."

Leaning over the bed, he gingerly folded the blanket back so he could see the baby's face. Young Bud looked unbelievably tiny to Cole who had never seen a baby this young before. His face was red, as wrinkled as an old man's. He was sleeping, his eyes glued shut, his little hands fisted above his head in what seemed an awkward position to Cole.

Cole stepped back, turning his gaze to Janet's amused face. "Why don't he relax? Is something wrong?"

"All tiny babies sleep that way." She looked at the baby's face. "He's the image of Bud, just the way I wanted him to be."

Cole nodded and asked, "How are you getting along with Sidonie?"

"She's wonderful," Janet answered. "I thought I'd hate her, like I hate Keldson and his mother. But I don't. Cole, I think she's Keldson's victim just as much as the rest of us are."

She was silent a moment, her eyes thoughtful. Then she said, "Is it wrong to hate Keldson? I keep remembering Bud, and how hard he worked on our ranch to make it pay so he could give more to me, and the baby when he knew it was coming. We were happy, and Keldson took it all away from us: Bud's life, the ranch, everything but the baby. I've got a right to hate him, haven't I?"

He looked down at her face which was growing tired. He thought of the bitterness that had been in him when Andy Carew died. Cole had lost a friend, but Janet had lost much more. Now even the baby would become a burden to her, without a husband, without money, without a job in a community where decent jobs for a woman were hard to find. Ben Davis, old and weathered, would in time become an additional burden. Yes, she had a right to be bitter and a right to hate.

He said, "You've got a right to hate him, Janet. But I don't think you do. You're too smart to spend much time being bitter."

She reached out and took his hand. "I've wondered about that. I've wondered sometimes if I was being loyal to Bud unless I did hate Keldson."

She was silent a few moments, her hand clasping his. "Funny how you've changed everything here, Cole. You've helped Ben

171

more than you'll ever know. You've helped me. He told me how you made the doctor come, how you practically kidnapped Mrs. Benson. I can't thank you. I just haven't got the words to tell you how I feel."

Suddenly uncomfortable, Cole was glad when Sidonie came in, wearing one of Janet's aprons. "You get out of here, mister. You're tiring her out with your talk."

Cole grinned. "Maybe I am at that."

Janet released his hand. "You come in here often. Promise?"

"I promise."

He wandered outside, sat down on the porch and smoked a cigarette, listening to the cricket who was starting his evening concert, and to the hot wind in the willows and cottonwoods along the creek. There had been no rain for weeks, and some of the wells in Cedar were going dry. People were coming to the creek for water.

Cole remembered something Ben Davis had said — that if Keldson could figure out a way to keep Big Horse Creek from running through the valley, he'd have things his own way. But that was something Marty Keldson couldn't do, even with Duke Le Clair and his entire Chain crew. Davis had said that no matter how long a drought lasted, Big Horse never went dry.

Sidonie came out of the house and sat down beside him. She didn't mention his fight with Keldson. Cole said, "I started to tell you about Andy. You want to hear the rest of it?"

She sat with her feet on the top step, hugging her knees, her eyes fixed on the mesa to the south, now only a vague line against the rapidly darkening sky. "Yes," she said. "That's why I came out."

"What was Andy like?" Cole asked. "The way you remember him?"

"I was just a child," she said. "I don't remember him very well."

"You must have been almost ten. You've got some idea what he was like."

Her voice softened. "He was tall, and very thin, almost gangling. I remember Dad saying that no matter how much food he stowed away, it all went to height instead of breadth. He was a fine rider. Dad said he made a good hand even if he was only a boy." She turned to look at Cole. "I'm not sure what I actually remember and what I've been told. Maybe Zelda tried to turn me against Andy."

"How do you mean?"

"I'm not sure, but I remember Andy as being quarrelsome. He was always fighting with Marty and he always got the blame. It's

173

why he left home. Dad took Marty's part every time. That's something I do remember."

"Marty always won the fights, didn't he?"

"Most of the time. How did you know?"

"Andy was the best friend I ever had. That's more than it sounds like because I've never had many friends. I've worked since I was twelve when my pa died. I cleaned stables and swamped saloons. When I got older, I got on as a deputy, and later I was marshal in a border town in Arizona named San Ramon. A man like me makes lots of enemies, but not many friends. That's why I say Andy was more than just an ordinary friend. When he was killed, I felt like I'd lost my right arm."

"Tell me about it," she said.

So he told her how it had been, the detective showing up in San Ramon and telling Andy that his father was sick, but Andy was to stay put until he was sent for.

"The man was lying," Sidonie said indignantly. "I don't know why, but he was lying. Dad wanted Andy home as soon as he could be found."

Cole nodded. "I figured it was that way, so I kept after him to go, but he wouldn't." He told her how Andy said he had a big row with his father who always took Marty's part to keep peace with Zelda, and how Andy worried about Sidonie because the detective said she was going to marry Marty, and finally how Andy was murdered. Then he asked, "Where was Duke Le Clair the first part of May?"

Sidonie considered a moment. "I don't know. He was gone. Marty said he was on a vacation."

"I think he was the one who killed Andy. I can't prove it, but it makes sense. He probably trailed the detective. Or maybe Marty got it out of your pa where Andy was after the detective got back here. Might be the detective was bought before he ever found Andy. That would account for him telling Andy to stay put."

"I can believe Le Clair did it," Sidonie said bitterly, "and that Marty paid him for it. But I can't believe Judge Benson —"

Cole looked at her gently, knowing this was not easy for her. He said, "I figured somebody on this range had to be responsible for Andy's death. I was pretty sure they'd get jumpy if they didn't know why I was here but knew I was interested in Andy, so I started asking for him."

"You stirred things up all right," she said.

"It was the only way I knew how to start," he said.

"Now you're in trouble," she said. "I'm sorry you got mixed up in it. It isn't your fight."

"You're wrong about that. Andy wanted somebody he could trust to look after you. I was his best friend just like he was mine. That's enough to make his fight my fight."

She stirred restlessly.

"Andy used to tell me about you," Cole went on. "He wanted to come back and see you, but he couldn't bring himself to do it as long as Zelda and Marty were still here. He was pretty bitter about your father always taking Marty's part against him."

Sidonie's voice was soft, almost nostalgic. "I remember I worshiped him the way any little girl would worship her big brother. I've been hoping he would come back, but I've never admitted it before, not even to myself."

She paused, then went on, "Cole, maybe I shouldn't say it, feeling the way I do about Zelda right now, but she's the one who's to blame for all the trouble we've had. I owe her a lot and I'm grateful, but —"

"Go on," Cole said. "Tell me about her."

"The first thing I remember about her was that she wanted things. I guess all of us want things, but she was different. Sort of greedy, like a child. I guess she'd gone so long without even the things she needed that she couldn't help herself when she had all the money she wanted.

"She bought silly things. She'd take the train at Placerville and go to Montrose or Grand Junction. Sometimes to Denver. When she got back, she'd be loaded with junk. Vases, gaudy silk runners for the table tops, figurines. Things like that. Then she began to collect jewelry. I'll bet she's got thousands of dollars' worth of jewelry in her room. She still wasn't satisfied, so she made Dad build the house."

"But Marty must have been the one who had Andy killed."

"I suppose so," Sidonie said, "but we have no way of knowing whether Zelda suggested it in the first place or not. She doesn't want to lose Chain. Or the house. It goes back to the way she used to live. She was a dancer, and when the people in town heard that they thought she was immoral. They didn't want to have anything to do with her. Sometimes I've felt she wants to get even with them.

"She used to move from one town to another when Marty was little. Rough places. Mining camps and railroad construction towns. She didn't earn much so they had to live in dirty hotel rooms usually near the railroad tracks. Marty played with the kids who lived around there. He learned that the way to keep from getting hit was to hit the other kid first. He was greedy, too. Like Zelda. I've heard him say a hundred times that the only things people respect are money and power and force."

"Benson told me your dad left Zelda his cash money," Cole said. "Looks like that would have satisfied her, seeing as she wasn't happy here."

"No, the money wasn't enough," Sidonie said. "Marty had his heart set on the ranch. When they didn't get a share of it, they were furious. Zelda's always talked like she expected Marty and me to get married. After Dad died, she worked a lot harder at it. I guess Marty just took it for granted I'd marry him. He never really courted me, but he kept other men away. At least he saw to it that none of them ever got serious. Sometimes he'd say, 'You'll come around. The Regulators'll gobble Chain up if I'm not here running the spread for you, and I won't keep on running it if you don't marry me.' Maybe I would have, in time, if you hadn't come along. I suppose I'd have drifted into it because there didn't seem to be anything else to do."

"No, you wouldn't," Cole said. "There's too much of Bill Carew in you to let you drift into anything."

"I'd like to think you're right," she said, "but I don't know. Zelda kept telling me Andy would make trouble if he ever did come back. Then when you came, she said Andy had sent you to make trouble, and that you'd take over if you had a chance."

"Andy did send me, but not in the way Zelda told you," Cole said somberly. "He was lying in the street when I got to him. He said, 'Go see if Sidonie's all right, Cole. Help her if she needs it.' Then he died in my arms."

Sidonie was silent, and suddenly Cole was aware that she was crying, staring out across the valley toward the mesa rim that was lost in darkness.

Cole put an arm around her shoulders and drew her against him. He held her that way for a long time until her weeping stopped. At last she said, "I'm glad you're here, Cole."

Chapter Sixteen

At breakfast the next morning Sidonie dropped a plate. The coffee cups rattled in their saucers as she placed them on the table. She seemed withdrawn, her face pale.

Suddenly she said, "I've got to see Janet and the baby," and ran from the room.

As soon as she was gone, Ben Davis asked, "What do you reckon's the matter with her? She's jumpy as a cat on a hot stove."

"It's my guess she's wondering if she done right coming here," Cole said.

Davis nodded. "I s'pose. She never knowed us except by sight, and for years she's heard we were Chain's enemies. She's thinkin' 'bout Marty and Zelda, an' what they'll do when they discover she ain't been home all night. Chances are she's scared."

"What can they do?"

Davis shrugged. "That's like tryin' to guess what the Colorado weather's goin' to be. Usually changes whilst you're lookin' at it. One thing you can be sure of — Marty won't take it lyin' down."

"Damned if I see what he can do. It's Sidonie's business if she wants to stay here."

Davis rose from the table and picked up his gloves. He crammed his shapeless, sawdust-covered hat on his head. "There's a couple o' things you ain't allowed for," he said. "First place, Keldson ain't used to bein' crossed. Second, he aims to marry Sidonie, come hell or high water. From what I hear, Zelda's been workin' on it ever since they were kids." He scratched an ear, scowling. "You can't blame Marty, far as that goes. She'll make any man a fine wife. She'd sure as hell make him a rich one. You put them things together an' you can see why Marty's goin' to steam when he finds her gone. Somethin' else, too. Chain's more'n money to him. It's people sayin' 'Yes sir' an' 'No sir' to him when they'd a heap rather spit in his face."

Davis walked to the back door. Turning, he added, "If I was you, Cole, I'd sure be some watchful today. If Marty can get on his feet after the whalin' you gave him, he might take it into his head to turn the town upside down lookin' for Sidonie. First man he'll come to will be you."

"I'll be watching for him," Cole promised.

181

He stayed at the table after Davis had gone, thinking of Andy. He remembered Andy telling him how wild Marty had been as a boy. "He'd lose that stinking temper of his at the drop of a hat. Most times, you didn't have to drop the hat. He'd start a fight for no reason at all, except that maybe he had to work his bad temper out on somebody, and I was always handy."

Marty the boy, as Andy had described him, and Marty the man were very much alike, Cole thought. Nor was this judgment his alone. The first night he'd talked to Sidonie she'd called Marty "unpredictable." And that was what Ben Davis had just said.

Sidonie came back, still nervous, but smiling now. "Janet's boy is a fine baby, Cole, isn't he? He hardly fusses at all. Right now he's having breakfast."

Cole said, "Sit down. I want to talk."

She sat, her smile fading. He reached across the table and took both her hands. "Are you afraid of what Marty might do because you didn't come home last night?"

"Zelda will worry," she said. "I should have sent word to them."

"You didn't answer my question."

She looked him straight in the eyes. "Yes, I'm afraid, but it's something else. I guess I'm mixed up. Can you understand that?"

Cole thought he could. Her eyes showed that she had spent a nearly sleepless night.

She had not seemed to doubt Cole last night when he'd told her why he was here. She was convinced that someone on this range had murdered Andy, and Marty Keldson must be her logical choice, having the most to gain from Andy's death.

So she was afraid of Marty, openly now. Yet she found it hard to turn her back on the only two people left in the world of those who had been her family, who represented the Chain that Bill Carew had spent his lifetime building.

It was her Chain, too. And all through the months of Bill Carew's illness, Zelda had impressed upon her that Marty was the only one that could hold it together against the Regulators who were waiting until Bill Carew died to move in and take their cut at it. It was only natural that she would find it hard to shed beliefs she had held so long.

Cole said, "Let's go see the Judge. It's time I told him why I'm here."

This seemed to ease her mind. She brightened. "All right, just wait until I tell Janet we're going."

Afterward they walked through the hot morning sunshine to Benson's office and climbed the outside stairs. Dry weather had held from the day of Cole's coming, and now Big Horse Creek was falling steadily, the peak of the run-off gone. Sidonie paused on the landing and looked across at the big house on the mesa, then at the distant peaks of the San Juans.

Cole, following her glance, saw the clouds nestled in the high troughs between the peaks. It would rain up there today, he thought, but it wouldn't help Chain range.

"This is the hottest, driest summer I've ever seen," Sidonie said. "It's rained everywhere but here."

They found Benson in his office, immaculate and pompous, exuding a fatherly good will as soon as he saw Sidonie. "You're in town early, my dear." He pulled up a chair for her and patted her back, ignoring Cole. "I've been meaning to drive out and see you but I've been busy."

She sat down, her hands folded on her lap. A ray of sun from the east window touched her face, bringing into sharp relief the lines of worry.

Cole walked to the window and rolled a cigarette.

Benson lighted a cigar, his chair creaking as he leaned back. He looked, Cole thought, like an antiquated saint, smugly convinced of his own righteousness. Cole began to grin with anticipation.

"What can I do for you, my dear?" Benson asked Sidonie.

She looked at Cole. "Tell him."

Cole said, "All right. But one question first. Is there any legal process by which Sidonie can take control of Chain?"

Benson refused to look at Cole. He said sharply, "There's no reason why she should. She'd never find a better foreman than Marty, and she can't run it herself."

"There are reasons — good ones," Cole said. "In the first place, Sidonie wouldn't have any trouble with the Regulators if she had control of Chain herself."

Benson put his cold-eyed stare on Cole. He said with the plain intention of being insulting, "You're promoting a job for yourself. Is that it?"

Cole held his temper with an effort. Benson looked back at the girl. "Sidonie, I'm sure Chain will have no trouble with the Regulators. If Bud Davis was alive it might be different. But with Walters running the show?" He shrugged contemptuously.

Sidonie said impatiently, "Cole, tell him why you're here."

"Yes, you do that," Benson said. "Tell me the story you've made this girl believe. It

185

should be a good one."

Cole crossed the room and yanked Benson to his feet. The man's face paled, and Cole threw him back into his chair. He said angrily, "I'm here because Andy Carew was shot in the back and killed. I'm here in your office this morning because I think you know who did it."

Benson's mouth fell open and the lighted cigar fell into his lap. He snatched it up and sat holding it, his hand trembling. No smugness about him now. His eyes were wide and suddenly very close to panic.

"You're lying," Benson whispered. "I spotted you for a crook the first day you hit town. Maybe you did know Andy. Maybe you played up to him, figuring some way or other to cut yourself a piece of cake. Now Sidonie's trying to make you foreman. What's next, making love to her? Or have you already done that?"

Cole reached for the Judge again, but Sidonie stopped him with her sharp, "Cole."

When he turned to her, her face was flaming. He looked for anger in her eyes, but found none.

"I don't know much about love," she said, "but since I've been in the Davis house, I've learned some things I didn't know. I've learned how good people can be, people who were supposed to be enemies of Chain. I've learned what those people think of Cole. So keep your accusations to yourself, Judge, and listen to what he has to say."

Benson threw his cigar into the brass spittoon at the end of the desk. "What proof have you got, Knapp?"

"Proof? Why, I was there. I was marshal of San Ramon, a little border town in Arizona. I was Andy's friend."

He paused, staring deliberately at the Judge until Benson looked away. Then Cole said, "A detective showed up. Said you'd sent him to find Andy. Only Andy wasn't supposed to come home. He was to wait for a wire telling him to come. After the detective left, I tried to talk Andy into coming, but he wouldn't. Said when he'd left home, he'd promised himself he wouldn't go back until his old man sent for him. A couple of weeks after that he was shot. Just long enough for a man to travel from here and do it if he hurried. I did some sign reading at the place where Andy was killed. I asked some questions afterward. I followed a trail and it led right here."

As he talked, Judge Benson's face turned gray. His hands were clenched on his desk. Cole looked him straight in the eyes. "How much do you know, Judge? How much did you have to do with it and how much did you get paid?"

"Nothing." Benson's voice rose until it was almost shrill. "Sure, I hired a detective to find Andy. Bill asked me to. He was sorry he'd let Andy go the way he had."

He took a linen handkerchief out of his pocket, his eyes asking Sidonie to confirm what he'd said. She turned to Cole. "The Judge is right. Dad began to see he'd made a bad mistake, giving Andy up for Zelda and Marty."

Benson nodded eagerly, as if wanting to clear himself of any part in Andy's murder. "Bill just wanted to find out where Andy was. It took the detective several weeks to find him. All we had to go on was a letter Andy had written to me from Tucson several years ago asking about Sidonie. I answered it, but nobody around here heard from him after that."

He mopped his forehead. "By the time the detective wired me his report, Bill had had a stroke and couldn't talk. Zelda wouldn't let me see him. So I told Marty and he promised to wire San Ramon and ask Andy to come home. We expected him here before Bill died. When he didn't come, I asked Marty and he said he'd sent the wire. I naturally figured Andy wasn't coming."

Benson rose and began to pace the room. "I should have wired Andy myself. I knew Marty hated him. I knew he wanted to marry Sidonie, and I knew if Andy did come, he'd run Marty off. I guess Marty knew that too. If the detective told Andy to wait, then Marty must have bribed him. Chances are, he wired Marty the same time he wired me."

He took out his handkerchief again and wiped his face. Cole, watching him, was not convinced. Benson had known something was wrong, all right. He just hadn't wanted to admit his guilty knowledge even to himself. It had been easier to go along, pretending to know nothing. Safer, too.

Sidonie looked at Cole. "What are we going to do now? How are we going to get Marty off Chain? I can't go back, knowing he was responsible for Andy's death."

"You don't have to," Cole said. "Stay right where you are."

"It must have been Duke Le Clair that Marty sent," Benson said reflectively. "He was gone when it happened."

Cole nodded. "Le Clair pretty well fits the description of the stranger that was in San Ramon at the time. I never got a good look at him. He stayed in his hotel room most of the time, but the clerk saw him. So did the waitress who took his meals to him."

"Judge, will you get word to Zelda that I'm all right?" Sidonie asked. "Tell her I'm taking care of Janet and the baby."

"You can stay with us." Benson returned to his chair, still shaken. "I don't know about getting control of your property, but I'll give it some thought."

"What about Keldson?" Cole demanded. "What are you going to do about him?"

Benson reached for a cigar and put it into his mouth, but he didn't light it. He stared at the top of his desk, then slowly raised his eyes to Cole. "I don't know, Knapp. I honestly don't know. He's sly and he's brutal and ruthless. You know that. He's planned on marrying Sidonie for a long time. Now there's no telling what he'll do. He might even destroy the town out of pure cussedness. He's always said that without Cedar the ranchers up the creek would be easier to handle."

"Will the Regulators help?"

"No," Benson said. "You can't expect help from anybody. That's the trouble. And I'm no better than Dusty Rhodes and the rest. We've seen what happens to men who fight Keldson. Bud Davis. You. And Andy." He looked up and spread his hands helplessly. "What can any of us do against a gunman like Duke Le Clair and Marty Keldson?" He chewed on his cigar a moment, then added uneasily, "Sidonie, you'd better get out of town for a while."

"No. There's got to be a way to stop him."

"If something would happen that'd bring the town and the Regulators together —" Benson frowned and shook his head. "Marty may do something terrible and foolish — Well, for your sake, Sidonie, I'd better go see Zelda. I'll tell her you're here because Janet needs you. Perhaps if I can convince her, she and Marty will at least let you alone."

Cole opened the door. Sidonie rose and walked toward it, pausing there and glancing back when Benson said, "I'm an old man, girl, but suddenly I feel like a free one. Knapp, you'll get no more opposition from me. We need a man like you."

Cole said, "I'll be around."

Sidonie left the office and Cole followed. When they reached the street, he said, "The Judge is in a corner. And a cornered rat will fight."

"Don't count on it from him." Sidonie was bitter as her eyes lifted to the house on the mesa. When they reached the bridge she said, "I suppose you find it hard to understand my part in this."

"No, I don't know what you could have done. You're an owner without control."

"I didn't try hard enough to use the influence I had," she said. "I didn't really understand. Dad never had much to do with me. He wasn't used to girls, and I guess I scared him. I was lonely. That's why I followed Andy around. And because I was a Carew, the other kids at school wouldn't play with me. Then Zelda came. She filled a need in my life. She made my clothes and taught me the things a girl should know, things my mother would have taught me if she'd lived."

She took a long breath. "It's hard to adjust to everything being turned around. They were always telling me that Bud Davis and his Regulators lived off us. Just lazy trash. Stealing our cattle — wanting to tear Chain down just because we were big."

She was silent the rest of the way to the house. Inside its doors, in the parlor's coolness, she said almost frantically, "I don't want to live with the Bensons, Cole, but I won't have any money of my own until I'm twenty-one, and I can't stay with Janet forever. She'll be well soon."

Janet called indignantly from the bedroom, "Sidonie, you can stay here as long as you want. Don't you know how much we owe you for coming when you did? We needed you. Mrs. Benson was about to drive me insane."

Cole grinned and Sidonie laughed. He said, "You see? Now stop worrying."

He started toward the back door, intending to head for the wood yard and give Ben Davis a hand with his work. He stopped as Sidonie called urgently to him from Janet's door.

"There's something I've got to tell you, Cole. I don't know whether it's important or not, but it probably is. I didn't think of it until the Judge said what he did about Marty destroying the town. He's up to something — at Stony Crest. Zelda let it slip. She said that when Marty got through at Stony Crest —"

But Cole was running through the door, remembering something he had heard. The night Janet's baby was born, Doc Holt had said something about being out at Stony Crest — about a man all smashed to hell by a rock that had fallen on him.

He didn't know much about Stony Crest except that it was somewhere at the other end of Triangle Mesa. But Davis would know. And after hearing what Zelda had said, he had a hunch they'd better get there fast.

Running toward the wood yard, he remembered the Judge's warning to Sidonie to get out of town.

Fear for her safety slowed his steps for a moment. But she would be safe in the house with Janet, at least safer than anywhere else. He went on, anger hardening his eyes and mouth.

Chapter Seventeen

Cole heard the whining saw bite into a cedar log before he was halfway to the wood yard. An instant passed, then he heard another block being lopped off. The screaming protest of the saw went on at regular intervals as Davis finished sawing the log he had on the supports.

Davis did not hear Cole approach, though Cole shouted at him. But he saw Cole as he turned to drag up another log. He motioned for Cole to pick up one end, but Cole shook his head. Davis looked puzzled, then walked over and disengaged the pulleys that drove the saw.

Cole motioned for Davis to shut down the engine. Davis hesitated, then shut off the engine and pulled the safety valve to release steam from the boiler.

When the hissing steam was gone, the sudden quiet was as disturbing as the noise had been. Cole shouted, "There's something going on out —" He stopped self-consciously, realizing there was no longer any need to shout. In a normal tone, he said, "I hate to stop your work, but Keldson's up to something at Stony Crest. I've got an idea where it is but I don't know exactly. Do you?"

"Sure." Davis motioned eastward. "It's at the other end of Triangle Mesa. What d'you figure he's up to?" As Davis talked, he raked the fire out of the steam tractor and extinguished the embers with a bucket full of water which stood near by.

"I don't know," Cole said. "Zelda let something slip to Sidonie yesterday. And Doc said something about a man being hurt out there the night I went after him to deliver Janet's baby. Said the man was all smashed to hell by a rock falling on him. I didn't give it much mind at the time because it could happen to anyone, anywhere. But now it looks to me like it's more'n just a rock slide that happened to catch some rider when he wasn't looking."

"What do you figure it is?"

"I don't know, but I think we'd better get up there."

Cole led the way at a brisk walk back toward the bridge, then he said, "Get your gun, Ben. I'll get a horse for you." Davis

196

nodded and went on to his house. Cole crossed the creek and strode on down the street to the livery stable. A scowling Dusty Rhodes brought Cole's horse and saddled a livery mount for Davis. Cole waited only a minute or two until Davis appeared, his gun belt buckled around his middle.

They stepped into their saddles and rode out of town. When the last building was behind them, Cole asked, "What is this Stony Crest?"

"Pile of rock. It's a ridge between Coroner and Big Horse creeks that ends up in a pile of naked rock. The ridge drops away from Stony Crest and turns into a kind of saddle that runs on into Triangle Mesa."

"What's the best way to get there?"

"Safest or closest?"

"Closest."

"Climb to the top of the mesa, then cut across it till you come to the east rim. They's a trail there that leads down to the saddle I was tellin' you 'bout. You cross that and you're right underneath Stony Crest."

"Come on then." Cole touched spurs to his horse's sides and lifted him to a lope. Davis's mount reluctantly maintained the same gait, though he lagged fifty feet behind.

When he hit the grade, Cole slowed his

horse to a walk, and Davis drummed on the livery stable horse's sides until the animal caught up.

Cole hipped around in the saddle and looked back. "What else do you know about Stony Crest, Ben?"

"Nothin' much. They's some funny colored streaks in the rock there. Was a time when some prospector figured them streaks meant gold. He cut a tunnel in solid rock for nigh to a hundred yards before he gave it up. Never found no gold. He was a fool for tryin'. Mistook bright yellow-colored sandstone for pay dirt."

"Tunnel still there?"

Davis shrugged. "Reckon so, though I ain't been near the place for years. Bud and me used to go there fishin' when he was younger an' afore he got married. Time or two he explored the tunnel, but it worried me to have him in there."

"Which direction does the tunnel go?"

"Straight through the ridge. If the prospector had stayed with it a little longer, he'd of put it right through to Coroner Creek."

Cole was silent, thinking, and he didn't like his thoughts. Then he said, "Let's put the things together that we know, just to see if you get the same idea I've got."

"Hop to it."

"Well, in the first place, we know Keldson is up to something at Stony Crest," Cole said. "Second, we know a man was hurt up there by a rock falling on him. Third, we know Keldson's given the Regulators a week to get out. Fourth, there's a prospect hole in the ridge between Big Horse and Coroner creeks that goes nearly all the way through. What does that add up to in your mind, Ben?"

"Nothin'. What does it mean to you?"

"You've seen the place," Cole answered. "You know how it lies and what it looks like, and I don't. But that tunnel's big enough to carry Big Horse Creek, isn't it?"

"Sure, if it was all the way through. I don't know how you'd get the water to it, though. It's ten feet above the level of the creek."

"Suppose Keldson was to dynamite Stony Crest? Suppose he dumped the whole thing down into Big Horse below the tunnel? Wouldn't that raise the water level so it'd run through the tunnel?"

Davis blew out a long, slow whistle. "Why, that dirty . . ." Cole waited. When Davis got through swearing, he said, "I can't believe that even Marty Keldson would be that ornery. Big Horse waters every one of the Regulators' spreads. Without it they'd go back to desert."

"How about the town?" Cole asked.

"It'd die, too. Look how many wells are dry right now. Take away Big Horse Creek an' they'd all go dry. They'd have to haul water all the way up the valley from the west end of Triangle Mesa."

They reached the top and Cole threw a long look at the Chain house. The yard was deserted except for a few white chickens. He spurred his horse, calling back, "How long a ride is it to Stony Crest?"

"Three–four hours from town. The way you're ridin' we'll make it in two."

"Good."

Cole rode on, giving his thoughts to Keldson, trying to figure a man who would ruin a dozen families and a town full of people. Once Stony Crest was dumped into Big Horse Creek, the thing was done. Removing thousands of tons of rock from the stream bed would be more than men could manage, would cost more than the entire valley of the Big Horse and the town of Cedar were worth.

Cedar would become a ghost town, and the ranches of the Regulators would become grazing lands for Chain cattle. No more would the hay grow green and tall. As time went on, the valley would become like a thousand other dry valleys in the west —

grazed down to the bare dirt until eventually the point was reached where little grew but deep-rooted greasewood that nothing could kill.

And above the town Keldson would look down and chuckle at the destruction his simple but ingenious plan had brought. But would he gain anything for himself? Or Chain? Anything but the right to look at a dead town and a dry valley, devoid of human life?

Cole shook his head, thinking there must be something more. For all of Keldson's brutality and ruthlessness, he was not a fool. Cole reined up and waited until Davis caught up. He said, "I've been thinking about this deal. If we've got it figured right, does Keldson stand to gain anything for Chain?"

"I've been thinkin' on it, too," Davis said. "There's several things he's got to gain, enough to make it worthwhile, I reckon." He motioned southward. "If it wasn't for the Regulators bein' in his way, he'd have a lot more range just for the takin'. You see, old Bill tried his damnedest to get hold of Big Horse Valley, but all he got was some hay land below town that wasn't much good. Maybe Marty figgers he can do somethin' Bill couldn't."

201

Cole nodded. That made sense. Marty Keldson had lived under the shadow of Bill Carew for a long time. He was the kind of man who would want to make his own reputation, and the quickest way to do that was to accomplish something Bill Carew had failed to do.

"Somethin' else, too," Davis went on. "Coroner Creek ain't big. Don't head up in the high country like Big Horse does, so it goes dry in real bad years and sometimes Chain gets caught short on hay. I remember more'n once Bill had to buy from the Regulators. They charged him plenty, you can bet, which is one reason he hated 'em like he done."

"And if Big Horse was running down Coroner Creek, Marty would always have a hay crop?"

"That's the size of it," Davis agreed.

Cole rode on, satisfied that he had the answer to his question. The two hours Davis had said it would take them dragged, but Cole was pressing his horse to the limit of endurance. Davis rode a hundred yards behind, having given up the battle to try and make the lazy livery stable mount stay up with Cole's horse.

At last, with the sun high in the sky, they reached the rim from which they could look down at Stony Crest. Cole halted his horse just back of the cliff and tied the reins to a sagebrush clump. Davis did the same. Afoot, they advanced to the rim.

The saddle Davis had mentioned was, Cole judged, about half the height of the mesa. But on beyond Stony Crest reared itself, naked, eroded rock, to almost the height at which they stood. Far below the summit of Stony Crest, Cole could see the miner's bore, a black spot near the base of the ridge.

Men worked down there, looking like ants at this distance. They toiled with stone boats and teams, hauling rock from the tunnel to the yellow-colored dump at the edge of the stream. To one side of the bore was a pile of wooden boxes, taller than a man, and almost ten feet across.

"Dynamite," Cole said, pointing. "There's enough yonder to put the whole ridge into the creek."

Davis's face was white. "You was right, Cole. The skunk really means to do it."

They returned to their horses and mounted. Cole said, "Go ahead, Ben. You know the trail and I don't."

Now Davis led out. For a time the trail was steep and sheer, mere shelf cut in the solid rock of the rim. Part of the time Cole's right foot in the stirrup was hanging over the edge.

Looking down, he realized what would happen to man and horse if the animal lost his footing.

Eventually they reached the talus slope, rode across it, and on into the cedar-covered ridges and gullies at its foot. From there they went across the swaybacked saddle, staying in the cedars, staying out of sight. At the far side of the saddle, a trail angled down into the canyon on the Big Horse side of the ridge.

Cole rode down it, keeping under cover of the cedars and piñon pine. A deer spooked away ahead of them. A jay scolded from a tree, and a gray squirrel chattered back at the jay. The sound of the stream was a rising roar, for here its drop was swift.

"Any fish in the creek?" Cole asked.

Davis swung his head and grinned. "You're damned right there's fish. Trout so big their heads stick out of the water when you scare 'em across the shallows."

"I'll remember that," Cole said.

Davis looked at him as if he were crazy. "Here we are headin' down there to jump a dozen men and you talk about fishin'."

"Those fellows aren't fighting men, Ben. And they're not Chain hands. They're laborers brought in by Keldson to do this job. Wonder how near they are to cuttin' their tunnel through?"

He got his answer as they picked their way across the small flat toward the mine dump, for one of the laborers ran out of the tunnel mouth, shouting, "It's through. I seen daylight on the other side."

Cole's eyes swept the small flat. On the far side of the tunnel were half a dozen tents, one of them larger than the rest. From the top of this one protruded a tin stovepipe, and the breeze brought Cole the smell of frying venison.

He dismounted, just as a man emerged from the big tent and began to beat on an iron triangle. Men streamed from the tunnel mouth. Others gathered from their tasks on the flat. Several wore guns, but they were belted high about their waists in the manner of men unaccustomed to their use.

They watched Cole and Davis with an odd wariness. Cole rode toward them, flanked by Davis, until one of the men who wore a gun and was obviously the foreman asked, "You Chain men?"

"Not us," Cole answered. The foreman dropped his hand toward his gun. Cole said sharply, "Don't," and the man's hand fell away. "That's better. Unbuckle your gun belt and let it drop. Tell the others to do the same."

The rest of the crew had stopped on their

way to the cook shack. Now they stood in a group, uneasily eyeing Cole and their foreman. The foreman, a big, hairy man whose blue work shirt was tight and dirty across his ample belly, blustered, "Listen here. You can't just ride in and —"

"Drop it," Cole said.

Slowly the foreman unbuckled the gun belt and let it drop. Cole said, "Now the others."

"Why? What the hell do you two want?"

"You're stopping work. Take your gear and get. You can stop by Chain on your way out of the country and pick up what's coming to you from Keldson."

"We don't know no Keldson."

"Le Clair then."

The foreman's muscles bunched. Cole said, "Don't try it, mister. I've got nothing against you personally, nothing against the others. You're doing a job you were hired to do. I'd hate to have to kill you."

Seconds dragged into a minute. Finally the foreman muttered, "What the hell? I ain't paid to die."

"That makes sense. Tell them to get rid of their guns."

The foreman turned. "We're knocking off. Shed your guns and leave 'em lay." He turned back to Cole. "This ain't over, friend. You still got to take this up with Le Clair. He'll be around like he is every day, and he won't be easy. He's the one that's paid to fight."

Cole didn't speak. He watched while the men sullenly let their gun belts drop. He called, "Go ahead and get your grub. Then start packing up. You're moving out."

When they had disappeared into the grub tent, Davis said nervously, "They might have a rifle stashed inside. Let's get out of sight."

Cole walked to the pile of dynamite boxes and sat down on one of them. "I doubt they'll shoot me now," he said, grinning.

Davis grinned back shakily. "What're you figurin' on doin' with all that stuff?"

Cole's grin widened. "I just got me a notion, Ben. We'll let these boys stay a little longer. I've got a job for them."

"Doin' what?"

"Packing the dynamite into the tunnel. We'll pile it up about halfway back, and then lead a fuse out here. We'll herd the men downstream about a mile and then light the fuse and take out for town. Must be two hundred boxes of dynamite here. We'll seal that bore until you won't know it's there, and that'll fix Keldson for good."

For a moment Davis stared at Cole, then

he began to grin. "Man, I like you more every day. Keldson'll go crazy when he sees what you've done."

"We'll bring him out into the open. That's sure, and it'll let the people of Cedar see what kind of man he is." Cole pushed back his hat and scratched his head. "Although I don't doubt but what they've known, really, all along. Up to now they've had no absolute proof because Marty's been careful and always laid the blame on someone else."

Talking, he had missed the rider coming down the trail. Now he looked up to see Duke Le Clair advancing toward him on a big gray horse. Le Clair held a rifle that was pointed steadily at Cole's chest.

The gunman's smile was small and without humor, his eyes cold. "So you figured it out." Cole nodded. LeClair purred, "Won't do you no good, friend. In a minute I'm going to pull this trigger. Then we'll throw you into the creek — you and your friend both."

Cole's smile widened. "Go ahead. Shoot. You'll be buried in a rock slide just like we will. Unless the concussion of the dynamite kills you before the rocks do. Be a hell of a way for a gunslinger to die, now wouldn't it?"

Le Clair's smile faded. He said without

208

conviction, "Bullets won't set dynamite off."

"Sometimes they don't," Cole conceded. "It's about fifty-fifty. Want to bet your life on those odds?"

The foreman burst out of the tent. "He's right. Don't chance it, Duke."

Cole said quietly, "I've got a proposition, Le Clair."

"What's that?"

"Throw your rifle down. Get off your horse. Then I'll step away from the dynamite and in front of the tunnel mouth." He paused, watching Le Clair, gauging the man's hesitancy. Then he added slowly and deliberately, "But I don't figure you've got the guts to do it. You see, I know how you shot Andy Carew."

Anger flickered in Le Clair's eyes, but he didn't speak.

And Cole prodded, "You shot Andy Carew, but you didn't have the guts to face even him. You shot him in the back. You're yellow, Le Clair. You're a gutless imitation of a badman."

Cole's prodding, along with some apparent uncertainty in Le Clair himself, brought the desired result. Fury was in the gunman's eyes, a killing fury that forgot all caution, all control. "Andy had

209

his chance but he wouldn't turn —"

He stopped. Cole began to grin, a tight, hard grin. He was sure at last. *This was the man who had murdered Andy Carew.* This was the man who had shot from ambush because he wanted all the odds his deceit could buy. If there had really been a challenge to turn, it had been only a formality, with not enough time for Andy to comply, otherwise the bullet would have entered his body from the front instead of from behind.

Le Clair was an assassin. Nothing more. Still, he would be fast when he was cornered, as he was now. Cole wondered suddenly where Keldson was. He should have been here at Stony Crest.

Then Cole promptly forgot Keldson. For here, before him, was the man who had killed his friend. There had been little doubt before. Now there was none.

Chapter Eighteen

Le Clair hesitated for a long time. Finally he reached a decision, and slipping the rifle into the boot, swung down from his horse.

The workmen had come from the tent, and now stood grouped, watching. Davis moved aside and drew his gun. Holding the men under it, he said, "Easy does it, boys. You ain't in this, so keep your hands in sight."

Le Clair moved behind his horse and slapped the animal sharply on the rump. The horse moved away. Le Clair said, "All right, Knapp."

Cole stepped aside carefully, keeping his balance, staying ready. The dynamite was still behind him, but he knew the instant he was clear Le Clair would draw and fire.

And Le Clair would know when Cole was clear a split second before Cole knew.

Again Cole took a careful step, his muscles tense. He'd faced gunmen before, yet today instinct warned him he'd never met one with the speed of this Le Clair. He took another step, stopped and watched the gunman's narrowed eyes. Not yet.

He moved again.

In mid-step, still facing Le Clair, he saw the man's eyelids twitch. Instantly Cole dived aside, snatching for the gun at his side.

Off balance, he felt the smooth, walnut grip of the gun. Then it was coming up, the hammer being eared back under the automatic pressure of his thumb.

He heard a yell, probably from Davis or one of the workmen. And he saw Le Clair's gun already level.

Black powder smoke billowed from Le Clair's gun muzzle. The bullet struck far back in the tunnel and ricocheted from wall to wall until the sound was lost in distance.

Cole squeezed the hair-spring trigger of his gun. He saw dust jump from the upper left hand pocket of Le Clair's vest. The gunman fired again, but this bullet struck the rocks high on Stony Crest, and started a rain of pebbles down the side of the cliff which did not reach the valley floor until Le Clair had begun to fall.

Surprise showed briefly in Le Clair's cold features. And then all expression left his face as he died.

He folded forward, his knees buckling under him. His face struck in the yellow dust, and he lay completely still, looking now almost like a sleeping boy instead of the killer he had been a moment before.

Cole stared at him like a sleep walker. Here was the end of the trail — here was revenge for the death of Andy Carew.

But he realized at once the job was not finished. Le Clair had been a paid assassin. Keldson had sent him, and Keldson had not yet paid for Andy's death.

Cole turned to the foreman and the crew of workmen. He said, "You've got one last job to do before you go. Carry that dynamite into the tunnel. Pile it up about halfway through. Then get to hell out. Start for town. Get a mile away from here as fast as your feet will carry you."

They stared at him, resentful and sullen, but they moved under the lash of Davis's harsh voice, "Get at it, damn you. Do what he says."

Cole stood motionless, watching the dynamite move, box by box, into the tunnel bore. The sun slid down the sky, westward toward the rim of Triangle Mesa. When the job was done, Cole asked the sweating men, "Can you carry your personal stuff?"

"Sure," the foreman said. "We'll put

packsaddles on the work horses."

"Do it then. And do it fast." Cole turned to Davis. "Keep your gun on 'em. I'm going into the tunnel."

He got a long coil of dynamite fuse and a couple of caps from a supply tent, and picked up a hammer and lantern. Lighting the lantern, he walked into the tunnel bore.

As soon as Cole left the entrance, he found the tunnel dark and dank. Its walls were of solid rock, showing only occasional streaks of the yellow sandstone the prospector had mistaken for gold. The floor was clean of rubble, and a path was worn there from the stoneboats and teams. There was no timber shoring to hold up the ceiling. None was needed. In this solid rock there was no danger of the ceiling collapsing.

Cole walked about fifty yards before he reached the pile of boxes. Putting down the lantern, he broke one of them open with his hammer. He took a cap from his pocket, a small, cylindrical tube of brass a little less than the thickness of a pencil and an inch and a half long.

With his pocket knife he cut the fuse end cleanly, and inserted it into the cap. With his teeth he crimped the brass cylinder so the fuse would not pull out. He took one of the dynamite sticks and peeled the paper away from the end, revealing a whitish, claylike substance that was the dynamite itself. He shoved the cap into the dynamite until it was buried, then replaced the waxed paper wrapping.

He buried the stick in the box beneath a dozen others, then laid two of the dynamite boxes on the fuse to hold it down so that he would not pull the cap free as he backed out of the tunnel.

Slinging the lantern over one arm, he backed out slowly, carefully uncoiling the roll of fuse as he went. When he reached the opening, the workmen were gone, traveling the trail toward the top of Triangle Mesa in frantic haste. Dust still hung in the air from their going.

Davis gestured toward Le Clair's body. "What about him?"

"Leave him here." Cole turned toward the fuse, then swung back. "No, let's sling him over the rump of my horse. I want to see Dusty Rhodes's face when we dump him off."

Together they lifted Le Clair's slight body to the horse's back and lashed him down. Cole said, "Mount up and get, Ben. I'll light the fuse and be right behind you."

Davis rode away. Cole stooped at the tunnel mouth and frayed the end of the fuse with his thumbnail. Then he struck a match. The fuse caught immediately and began to spit fire.

Cole gave a last look at the scene, wondering what Keldson would do when he heard about what had happened today. He was sure of only one thing. Keldson would hold Cole responsible, and would strike back at once. He knew by now he had lost Sidonie. Then this! There would be no more halfway measures. Whatever he did, the finish would not be more than hours away.

Cole mounted and rode up the trail after Davis. They passed the workmen where the trail mounted toward the top of the mesa. They negotiated the shelf in the rimrock, and halted their panting horses at the top.

Cole was grinning now. He said, "Hold tight to your horse's reins, Ben. He'll want to run in a minute."

He looked at the scene below, the cluster of tents, the scattered stoneboats and harness, the black, gaping mouth of the tunnel. The sound came to him as vibration first, beneath his feet, and his horse snorted and pulled against the reins. Cole held on.

Then he saw the smoke and dust pour from the tunnel's mouth like smoke billowing from a cigar smoker's mouth. After that, by almost thirty seconds, he heard the sound, a dull, sustained roar that seemed to last a full minute.

The rocks at the top of Stony Crest began to move, to settle. A few closest to the gorge broke loose and tumbled ponderously to the bottom where they smashed the tents and rolled on across the flat and the scattered gear.

Great clouds of dust rose from their falling, and for almost ten minutes totally obscured the scene. But the breeze from the east rolled them away, and finally Cole and Davis could see their handiwork in the last afternoon sunlight.

The flat was gone, covered by a jumbled mass of broken rock. The tents had disappeared, and there was no evidence that a tunnel had ever existed. The dynamite had dropped the mountain into it.

A few of the falling rocks had gone into the stream to form a dam. Water was already backing up behind it. For a day, maybe less, there would be only a trickle in Big Horse Creek. After that, it would overflow the dam and would run again through the Regulators' meadows, through the town of Cedar.

Cole sighed with relief. "Time to be getting home, Ben. Supper's going to get cold."

Davis gave him a wondering stare. He said with frank admiration, "Man, you beat the Dutch."

"Then let's hope Keldson's Dutch. I figure we'll be hearing from him soon."

The sun was setting beyond the rim of Triangle Mesa, and was blinding and brassy in Cole's eyes. He tipped his hat forward to shield his eyes from the glare. Far beyond the end of the mesa, almost lost in the haze, he could barely make out the La Sal Mountains, and the clouds that hung there.

For the first time in many weeks there was a kind of peace in Cole. Part of his job was done. Le Clair, Andy Carew's actual murderer, was dead. Keldson's plan to ruin the valley and the town and to increase the flow in Coroner Creek was spoiled.

But what of Keldson himself? Cole was not able to free his mind of the thought he'd had before he'd left the bottom of the canyon: Keldson would strike back as soon as he heard what had happened. He would hear sometime tonight when the first of the workmen reached Chain.

Davis must have been thinking the same thing for he said, "Cole, looks to me like we ought to do somethin' 'bout Janet and Sidonie. Maybe get 'em out of town. No tellin' what Keldson will do when he finds out about this."

Cole said, "We'll see. We'll see," and sank his spurs into his horse's side.

Chapter Nineteen

The sun sank behind the La Sals to the west, and Janet Davis's kitchen filled with the savory smells of roast beef and baking potatoes, a meal that could be kept hot without spoiling for hours. Coffee bubbled on the stove.

The baby woke and cried, and Janet went to feed him. Afterward, with dusk settling over the town, she returned with the lighted lamp, and sat down to help Sidonie keep her lonely vigil.

At last — at last they heard the sound of voices, and a moment later the stamp of booted feet on the porch.

Sidonie jumped up and ran to fling the door open. Cole came in, dusty, tired, but grinning. Impulsively Sidonie threw her arms around him and hugged him. Davis ducked around them and opened the oven door to sniff its contents.

Sidonie pulled away. "I was worried about you. What happened?"

Cole drew her to him. "It makes me feel good to have you worrying about me." He released her, adding, "Dish up the grub and I'll tell you about it while we eat."

He washed and combed his hair, and coming to the table, dropped into a chair. There was hunger in his eyes she had not seen before. Suddenly the foreboding of the day was gone. She set the table, and humming, began to lay the food upon it.

Davis came in and sat down. As they ate, Cole told what had happened. It was good, Sidonie thought. They had saved the valley and the town. More than that, they had kept Chain from being blamed for something she would have been ashamed of all her life.

But as they went on talking, the smile faded from Sidonie's lips, the pleasure Cole's return had brought to her was replaced by the old foreboding, the old fear. She knew, and surely they must, too, that they had spent the day prodding a rattler with a stick. And tonight, or tomorrow, the rattler would strike.

Chapter Twenty

Cole and Ben Davis were tired, but they ate quickly, both knowing they had no time to sleep or rest. Keldson would be on the move when the first of the straggling workmen reached Chain.

Cole asked himself what Keldson would do when he got the news, but he could not answer his own question. It was like trying to guess where summer lightning would strike next. You couldn't tell where; you only knew it would.

He smiled reassurance at the two girls as he left. "Don't worry about us." He sensed that Sidonie did not want him to leave, but she made no effort to stop him. She followed him to the door.

Davis had already gone out to the horses, but Cole paused, looking down at the girl and thinking how the picture had been completely changed during the last few hours. He said, "Keldson's going to be looking for you, too. Chances are Zelda's told him to fetch you back to Chain no matter what else he does. Can you use a gun?"

She nodded. "I'm a good shot."

"Ben's got his revolver, but I know there's a rifle here. Maybe Janet's got another gun. Keep 'em handy and don't let Keldson come in if he shows up."

"We'll be all right." She looked directly at him. "You just see you take care of yourself, Cole."

He wheeled without another word and left at a hard walk. He mounted, his horse still holding Le Clair's body, and rode to the bridge. He crossed, looked at the town and wondered what it would be like after this night.

When Cole and Davis reached the livery stable, Dusty Rhodes was just returning from supper. A toothpick dangled from the corner of his mouth.

Cole called, "Marshal, I've got something for you. Go inside and light a lantern."

Rhodes swung around, recognized the lumped shape across the rump of Cole's horse as a body, and immediately scuttled into the stable. When Cole led his horse in, the lighted lantern hung from a nail in the wall, and Rhodes faced him, a double-barreled shotgun in his hands.

"Put that damned thing down," Cole said in disgust.

"Not till I find out what this is all about," Rhodes said, his voice so high it cracked.

Cole walked to the man and snatched the shotgun from the marshal's hands. He broke it and angrily threw it into the shadows.

He untied Le Clair's body and eased it to the ground. When Rhodes saw who it was, an involuntary cry broke out of him. "You bushwhacked him!"

"The hell I did," Cole said grimly. "Look at the hole in his vest. I've got a dozen witnesses that'll testify he drew first. Ben here is one of 'em."

"Ain't possible," Rhodes muttered.

"Maybe not," Davis said, "but that's the way it was."

Cole looked at Rhodes, contempt in his face. "Better hop over the fence, marshal. You're on the wrong side."

"Wait till Keldson —" Rhodes's voice trailed off.

"We're waiting," Cole said, "and we're going to be ready for him. Was I you, marshal, I'd fork one of the horses you got here and hightail out of the country. In the meantime, saddle us a couple of fresh horses."

"What're you going to do?"

Sudden anger rose in Cole. "Damn you,

get those horses. We're going to do a job you should have done six months ago."

Rhodes disappeared into a stall in the rear of the barn. He returned with two bays, and Cole and Davis transferred their saddles and bridles to the fresh mounts. Cole said, "Rub those other two down before you leave."

He didn't know whether Rhodes would or not. The man was scared. But it didn't matter — the horses weren't so hot they wouldn't cool off safely. He stepped into the saddle and rode out, Davis following close behind.

They headed upcountry in the direction of the Regulators' spreads. Nothing would have warned them so far. The creek would be going down because of the dam at Stony Crest, but that probably wouldn't have been noticeable before sundown, and it was dark now. So it was up to Cole and Ben Davis.

They rode hard and fast, sparing neither themselves nor their horses. They passed up the spreads nearest town and rode to the head of the valley, to the last ranch at its upper end.

Nearing it, Cole said, "Let's split up, Ben. We'll cover more territory that way. You warn that upper place and I'll catch the next one down. Then you get every other one all the way back to town. Tell 'em what happened and what Keldson was trying to do. Tell 'em what we did and let 'em figure out for themselves what he'll do next."

Davis grunted agreement and galloped toward the one-room shack, its window showing the light of a lamp. Cole turned in at the second place down. The man who answered his hail was a stranger to him. Behind the rancher Cole could see his wife, a plain, middle-aged woman, and several children ranging in size from toddlers to kids of ten or twelve.

Cole said, "My name's Knapp," and quickly told what had happened at Stony Crest. He finished with, "If you men have never worked together before, you'd better do it tonight."

There was fear in the woman's eyes. The man was scared, too, but he tried not to show it in front of his family. Cole said, "Ease up, mister. Maybe nothing will happen. But you've got a better chance of keeping Keldson from cleaning you out if you get together now."

"I've heard of you," the man said. "You'll lead us?"

"Yes, if that's what you want," Cole answered. "But I've got to get back to town. You get a move on and warn the others as you go. I want to see you all together when you get into Cedar."

He wheeled his horse back to the road, thinking suddenly of town and wondering if he had made a mistake coming up here. He thought of Sidonie, and of Janet and her tiny baby. Keldson knew Sidonie was in town, and if he thought Cole was there, too, he might ignore the Regulators entirely, believing that if the town was destroyed, the upcountry ranchers would run without a fight.

Cole intercepted Davis on the road, riding with another man Cole could not identify in the dark. Cole said, "I got a notion we played this wrong, Ben. We've opened the game. Let's get back to town and let these men warn each other. I'm worried about —"

"Janet?"

"Both of 'em. I figured Keldson would hit the valley first. But now I'm thinking I was wrong. A burning town might throw a scare into the ranchers."

Before he finished Davis had drummed his horse into a hard gallop. Cole followed, finding to his satisfaction that the livery stable horses, fat on grain and lazy, ran better toward town than away from it. Together they thundered down the road, while behind them the nucleus of Regulators grew as each rancher was warned.

Though they were unsparing of their horses, it seemed to Cole that it took an eternity for him and Davis to reach Cedar. He sighed in relief when he saw the town's lights before him.

"Ring the fire bell, Ben," Cole said. "I've got a hunch we're running out of time."

Davis veered away from him. Cole slowed his horse, throwing a glance at the Davis house across the creek. He realized more than ever that Sidonie's safety was the most important consideration to him personally; but he could not forget that he had started this, and there were other people to consider. So he followed Davis, reining to a stop just as the bell began to toll.

Doors opened and people ran into the street. A few men, members of Cedar's volunteer fire department, came running in various stages of undress.

"Where's the fire?" a man yelled.

And another, "What's going on?"

Cole waited until a dozen or more had gathered. Many carried lanterns, so he was able to identify most of them. Judge Benson wasn't there. Neither was Doc Holt nor Dusty Rhodes.

He said loudly, his voice carrying the

length of the block, "This is a long story, but I'll make it short. You've wondered who I am and now I can tell you. I used to be marshal of San Ramon in Arizona. Andy Carew was my friend. Keldson sent Le Clair to murder him. I followed him here."

A murmur swept through the crowd. The storekeeper, Jake Reynolds, called, "You're trying to tell us you trailed Le Clair all the way from Arizona?"

"That's right. Trouble was, I'd never seen Le Clair when he was in San Ramon because he was damned careful to keep out of my sight, so I couldn't be sure. The only way I knew how to smoke my men out was to ask around for Andy. I smoked 'em out all right, Le Clair and Keldson both."

He paused. He saw doubt in their upturned faces, then fear and anger. They had lived on the same range with Marty Keldson for years. They knew what he had done and what he would do again, and it was natural for them to blame Cole for bringing trouble upon them. And Keldson, in their minds, was a synonym for trouble.

"Today Ben Davis and me went to Stony Crest," Cole hurried on. "Keldson had a work crew there. They'd just finished running that miner's tunnel clean through from Big Horse to Coroner Creek. They had a couple hundred cases of dynamite on hand, figuring to blow Stony Crest down into Big Horse Creek and force the water through the bore into Coroner. He aimed to dry up your valley and your town, and let the dryness drive you out. Since I've been here, I've heard it said Keldson claims there's no use for Cedar to exist. That's the way he meant to destroy you, and he'd have done it if Ben and me hadn't got there when we did."

The murmur of voices grew until it was an angry rumble. All of them knew what Keldson thought of them and what he had threatened, and they knew he was capable of doing the very thing Cole had said he intended to do.

Cole held up a hand, shouting, "No sense talking about what you're going to do. We've already done it. I made Keldson's crew carry the dynamite into the tunnel and I blew it up. Big Horse is going to slow down to a trickle because of the rock and dirt that went into the creek, but it wasn't much of a dam. By tomorrow night you'll have as much water running through town as you had this morning."

"What about Keldson?" Reynolds called.

The blacksmith, Tom Binn, added his voice, "And Le Clair?"

"Le Clair's dead. Keldson's the man

we've got to take care of. That's why Ben rang the fire bell. By now Keldson must know what's happened. No telling what he'll try. Maybe burn your town. Maybe he'll settle for burning out the valley. All we know is that a man who would destroy your town by taking away your water supply will do anything, so we've got to be ready."

Silence now, the silence that crawling fear brings to men when they understand what they face. This wasn't like the fear he had seen in their faces a moment before; no anger, no resentment, for this was a fear that went far deeper. Now they knew they would have been destroyed if Cole had not smashed Keldson's plan; and they knew equally well that Keldson would still destroy them if he could.

Cole saw Judge Benson coming from the bridge, tucking his nightshirt into his hastily donned pants. His hands shook as he came up to the edge of the crowd. He licked his lips, tried to clear his throat, but seemed incapable of saying anything.

Fear, Cole knew, was a contagious thing, and in a moment it would infect the whole crowd and panic would destroy any chance the town had of defending itself.

Cole raised his voice angrily. "Tonight you're going to find out something. You'll find out if there's any guts left in you. If there isn't, then I'll be damned if you're worth worrying over. If you won't fight now, you never will."

He looked straight at Benson. "You got anything special to be scared about, Judge?"

Benson cleared his throat. This time he was able to speak, and now there was no arrogance in him. "Fire! Up the valley. Above Walters's place, it looked like. I saw the glow from my bedroom window."

Cole felt a sinking sensation in his stomach. Keldson had started. He'd sweep the valley clean and he'd hit the town, and if his fury hadn't spent itself, he'd burn the town itself. Cole's thoughts turned to Sidonie. Keldson would tear Cedar apart until he found her, and when he did . . . But Cole could not think beyond that point. He only knew that it must not be allowed to happen.

Chapter Twenty-one

Cole looked at the white and frightened faces before him. He said wearily, "Time to choose, boys. You're going to have to decide whether to run or fight. I can't decide it for you. Ben Davis and me are going to stay. So's the Judge. So's Dusty Rhodes if he's still in town. They're all the law there is, and I'm going to see they stay. The rest of you do what you think is best, but I'll tell you this — if you can be run out of this town, you can be run out of any town. Think it over."

He turned away, glancing again at the Davis house across the creek. Ben Davis stood behind him, waiting, his contemptuous gaze on the crowd in the street.

"Judge, you're going to have to let the women and kids stay in your place till this is over," Cole said. "The ones that aren't running, I mean. Your house is brick, so it won't burn. Ben, take our horses to the livery stable. See to it that Janet and Sidonie and the baby get over to the Judge's house. Then come back."

Cole stepped down into the crowd and grasped Benson's arm. "Come on, Judge. We're going to find Rhodes. You two have let Keldson run things long enough. Now let's see what we can do about it."

Behind Cole someone yelled, "Knapp."

Cole turned. The man who had called was the blacksmith, Tom Binn. He said in a lower, less certain voice, "How do you know we're really going to have trouble? You're guessing, ain't you?"

"You heard the Judge say he'd seen a fire up the valley," Cole answered.

"Might have been an accident," Binn said doggedly. "We don't know Keldson set it. Or even if he did, we don't know he's fixing to hurt us."

"You stay," Cole said. "You stay and find out."

He started to turn to Benson again when a voice said, "I've got the answer to that question." A man pushed through the crowd. It took Cole a moment to recognize the battered, blood-smeared face — the foreman of the crew that Cole and Davis had run out of the canyon below Stony Crest.

"What are you doing here?" Cole demanded.

"Had to warn you," the man said. "Keldson wouldn't even pay us our wages. Blamed me for what happened. Beat hell out of me. Said he was gonna burn this town and clean out the valley. He ran us off. The last we knew his crew was getting ready to ride."

"Where's the rest of your crew?"

"Headed down the creek, but I figured you ought to know. I want a gun. I aim to get a crack at 'em when they hit this burg."

"You'll get one," Cole said. "What's your name?"

"Lynn. Frank Lynn."

Cole shook hands with him. "Thanks for coming. Now you hike over to the Staghorn and get yourself a drink. I reckon we've got some time yet." As the foreman walked away, Cole swung back to Tom Binn. "You got your answer. What about it?"

"I got one answer," the blacksmith said, "but I reckon we need another one. Suppose we do stay? What chance we got?"

He could expect this question, too, Cole thought. They were timid men who had put up first with Bill Carew's domineering rule and then Keldson's until it had become a habit. "You've got a chance to fight for what's yours," Cole said in disgust. "A chance to stand up and show Keldson you're men. That ought to be enough."

"I mean what chance we got of stopping him."

"No chance at all if you're going to run the first time things get tough. A good chance if you stand and fight. Keldson's only a man, like Le Clair was. He can die like any man. Or he can be made to tuck his tail between his legs and run. I'll tell you one thing, though. A thousand rabbits can't whip a wolf. So if you're going to be rabbits, you'd better run."

A man's voice raised above the mutter of the crowd, "You can't talk to us like that, Knapp. Who the hell do you think you are?"

Cole placed that one. Al Sands, the hotel owner. He grabbed the man by the front of the nightshirt and yanked him close. "I'll talk to you any damned way I please. We've got to find out if there are any men left in this town."

Sands jerked away angrily, his eyes meeting Cole's defiantly. The crowd behind the hotel owner was beginning to grow indignant, the mutter of voices raised to a low rumble. "All right," Cole yelled. "Make up your minds. Who's running and who's staying?"

"I'm staying," Sands said, "if only for the pleasure of smashing you in the face when this is over."

Others joined him: Reynolds, Tom Binn, and several Cole didn't know. Others slunk away to hurry home and get ready to run. But Cole had enough to make a fight of it, ten counting himself and Davis, and not counting Benson and Rhodes who would be lightweights at best.

"All right," Cole said, "you boys go home and tell your families to get over to the Judge's house. Have 'em pick up all the grub they can lay their hands on quick. Hard to tell how long this'll last, so tell 'em to stay inside no matter what happens. You boys fetch back whatever guns and ammunition you've got. If there's not enough, Reynolds will have to open up his store. Come back here and I'll tell you what to do."

They stood staring at him a moment. He swept a hand out in an angry motion. "Move, damn it. You think Keldson's going to squat on his hunkers all night?"

They went on the run. In an instant the street was empty. Cole grasped Benson's arm again, but the Judge jerked away with a slight return of his old dignity. "You don't have to drag me."

"All right, then drag yourself."

"This is your fault," Benson said. "Not mine."

"I'd expect you to say that, but you're

wrong and you know it. A breakdown in the law is the fault of the men who take the people's money for enforcing it. Ever think of that?"

Benson didn't answer as he hurried toward the livery stable beside Cole. Finally he said, "You're right, but what are we going to do?"

"We've got twelve men here in town," Cole said with exaggerated patience. "We'll have more when the Regulators get here. We can fight the Chain crew and win. That's what we're going to do."

"But these men in town — they're not fighting men."

"Neither were the men at Bull Run — or Gettysburg, but they fought like hell just the same."

The Judge was silent. They reached the stable and caught Rhodes as he was mounting his horse. Cole grasped the bridle. "Get down, marshal."

"You told me to get out of town," Rhodes said aggrievedly. "That's what I was aiming to do."

"I've changed my mind," Cole said. "You're mighty poor stuff for a lawman, but you're the best we've got. What we do tonight is going to be done in the name of the law. Now get down off that horse."

Rhodes slid to the ground, removed the saddle, and led the animal back to a stall. When he returned, Cole motioned him and Benson into the street. Lanterns glowed from one end to the other, all moving toward the bridge and Judge Benson's house.

A baby cried. A little girl screamed as she fell and skinned a knee. Most of the people in the procession were silent, shocked by fear and the suddenness of what had happened.

A woman sobbed at leaving her house. She kept crying out, "I've got to take my things, Sam. They're all we've got in the world." But her husband pulled her on.

Benson asked, "You really think Keldson's crazy enough to burn a whole town?"

"He's not crazy," Cole answered. "That's been proved to me ever since I've been here. He's mean and unpredictable, and right now he's mad. He figured he had this valley whipped without raising a hand. Now he knows he was wrong, so he might do anything."

Benson was silent. Cole said, "What about it? You know Keldson better'n I do. Am I right or wrong?"

"You're right," Benson answered. "Marty isn't worried about the law, with Dusty here eating out of his hand."

"You're a good one to talk," Rhodes whimpered.

"The sheriff's a long ways from here," Benson went on as if he hadn't heard. "He didn't come when Bud Davis was killed. I'm not sure he'd come if Cedar was burned to the ground. Even if Marty had succeeded in diverting Big Horse, I doubt that the sheriff would have bothered to come. That's the way it's been ever since the present sheriff got into office. This end of the county is no-man's land as far as law enforcement goes. We don't have enough votes to matter one way or the other."

They walked up the street toward the fire bell where the townsmen were gathering. Then Benson said, "Marty will do something more than burn a few haystacks, but I'm not sure he'll wipe out the town. Don't seem to me he's got enough to gain."

"Well, what will he do?" Cole demanded.

"I don't know, but there is one thing you've got to remember. Sidonie is still the key to Chain. He wanted to marry her. I guess by now he knows she'll never have him. But if there's a big fight here in town, and she's killed —"

Benson's voice trailed off. Cole said, "If she dies, Chain goes to Zelda, and Marty will inherit from her. Be easy to make it look

239

like Sidonie's death was an accident, with bullets flying around. That what you're thinking, Judge?"

"That's it," Benson said heavily. "I told her the other day she ought to leave. Now it's too late."

"No, it's not too late," Cole said. "Keldson won't get his hands on her. I'll make sure he doesn't."

Chapter Twenty-two

They reached the fire bell. Cole made a cigarette and hunkered against the wall of a
building, waiting until all the men who had
promised to come were here. Now Cole could
hear the sounds of wagons leaving town, the
popping of whips, the shrill cries of the team-
sters.

Hastily loaded wagons rolled by, heading
down Big Horse Creek toward the San
Miguel. One man hurried past pushing a
wheelbarrow, piled high and overbalanced,
but he kept it moving. His wife and two children plodded behind him. Others walked,
their most valuable possessions strapped to
their backs or carried in their hands.

Sight of the exodus had a disturbing effect
on the men waiting beside Cole. It seemed
to anger them, but it frightened them and
made them doubtful, too.

Cole got up and stepped away from the
wall. He shouted to be heard over the racket

in the street. "Two of you go to the upper end of town. Find a place to hide where you can see the road. If Keldson shows up, fire two shots apiece. But don't get trigger happy. I'm counting on Walters and his Regulators."

When nobody moved, Cole jabbed a finger at Al Sands. "You." He motioned to the man beside the hotel owner. "And you. Move."

After they trudged away, Cole said, "The rest of you split up on both sides of the street, half on one side, half on the other. Pick yourselves places in the buildings on Main. Don't fire till I give the word. We don't want to dump Walters and his men out of their saddles if they should happen to ride in first."

Cole turned to Rhodes. "You and the Judge stick here. You've always claimed you didn't have any evidence against Keldson. You'll have it before sunup if I'm guessing right, enough to send him to Canyon City for fifty years. Arrest him, Dusty. You might still have a chance to keep your job."

Rhodes was silent, but the blacksmith Tom Binn laughed. "I didn't think any man could joke when he's in the tight spot you're in, Knapp, but talking 'bout Dusty arresting

Marty Keldson is a joke if I ever heard one."

"Maybe not," Cole said. "All depends on how this shapes up. Keldson doesn't have Le Clair. Might be he'll make a mistake, a bad one." Cole jerked his head at Davis who had returned from Benson's house. "Come on. I want to see how things look on the other side of the creek."

Together they crossed the bridge and walked along the road past the dark Davis house to Benson's place, now blazing with a lamp in every room. Sidonie was on the porch, a rifle in her hands. She called, "Who is it?"

"Me an' Ben," Cole answered.

She leaned the rifle against the wall as Cole and Davis stepped up on the porch. Cole heard her breathing as he stopped a few feet from her, but her face was a soft blur in the moonlight. He was unable to see her expression, but he was glad to have found her this way, standing guard with a rifle.

"Ben, go in and tell them to pull the shades and blow out all the lamps they can do without. Have them stay away from the windows and get them busy fixing grub for the men back there. Keldson might show up in half a minute, but it might not be for hours."

Davis disappeared inside. Cole looked at Sidonie, sensing fear in her and wishing there was some way he could reassure her.

He took her hands and found them cold. He felt a sudden desire to take her into his arms, but this was not the time. He released her hands instead and stepped back.

"This will be over tomorrow," Cole said.

She did not reply. Instead, she seemed suddenly and strangely angry with him. "You're made of iron, Cole Knapp. Go on back to your fight. When it's over, go back to your drifting."

She whirled to go into the house, but Cole caught her around the waist. Her hair was soft against his face. He said gently, "Wait a minute now. I'm done drifting. I'm staying here."

She turned in his arms and her lips touched his. He brought her to him, his grip hard and possessive, and he kissed her as though afraid he would never have a chance again. She pressed against him, her arms tight around him.

Ben Davis chose that moment to open the door and come out on the porch. He cleared his throat noisily. Cole moved back, Sidonie letting him go.

"They're workin'," Davis said. "That

hatchet-faced Mrs. Benson is crackin' the whip."

Cole stepped down off the porch and spoke to Sidonie, "Have Ben tell me when the grub's ready. I'll send some men over to fetch it."

"All right, Cole," she said, and her voice was soft.

He walked toward the bridge, less sure of himself than he'd let anyone know. The townsmen were at a disadvantage. They assumed Keldson would ride in openly, but Cole wasn't sure he would. Suppose Keldson's men filtered into town one at a time? Or what if they fired a few buildings and then withdrew?

Cole knew what would happen. Nothing could hold the townsmen in line. They'd forget Keldson and fight the fire. And when Keldson came a second time, he'd find them with buckets in their hands instead of rifles. In the light of the fire, Chain guns would cut them down like a sharp sickle slashing through ripe grain.

Cole prowled the rim of the town, silent as a shadow, stopping often to listen. He eluded the guards at the upper end of town with ease. Because he did, he knew how easy it would be for Keldson to do the same.

He went on around the other side of town,

and down to its lower end where he watched the last of the fleeing refugees pull a buggy along the road by hand. It was loaded high with household goods. A man pulled on one shaft, his wife on the other, three kids trudging behind. Cole wondered what they would do if the town survived. Would they come crawling back to the homes they had lacked the courage to defend?

Cole let them pass and crossed Main again. He thought he heard a sound in the direction of Davis's wood yard, and stopped to listen. He stood motionless for several minutes, but heard nothing more.

Time for Walters and his Regulators to arrive. Past time. They should have been here an hour ago. Cole's forehead creased with worry as he glanced up the valley, and for the first time saw the orange tint of flame reflected against the sky. Another ranch house burning. Or a haystack. It didn't matter so long as the occupants had escaped with their lives. Haystacks could be replaced, houses rebuilt. Sidonie would be generous, he knew, once she controlled Chain again.

He returned along Main, clinging to the shadows, and at last reached the upper end. He shouted, "This is Knapp. Call out your names and where you are."

"Reynolds, second story window of the

246

hotel." Then more plaintively the store-keeper asked, "Where the hell is Walters and his bunch?"

Cole didn't answer. Now the others were singing out names and positions. Cole admitted they had placed themselves well. He went on.

His lookouts called to him from the shadows at the upper edge of town. He talked with Al Sands for a minute or two, finding that he had lost his belligerence.

From somewhere down the street Davis yelled, "Grub's ready," and Cole walked that way. He selected Reynolds from the hotel and Tom Binn to help Davis bring the food and distribute it. Then, rolling a cigarette, he sat down against the wall of the store and touched a match to his smoke. He shielded its glow with his cupped hands and waited.

Davis and the other two returned with plates, cups, food, and coffee. Cole took coffee, nothing more. The food was finished, and still the waiting went on. Cole studied the eastern horizon but could detect no hint of dawn.

And then, at last, he heard a shot — not two from each guard, but a single shot.

He was on his feet instantly and running. A single shot!

His gun was in his hand, though he had no recollection of drawing it. And tension was in him, the tension of long, fruitless waiting that now, perhaps, was finally at an end.

Chapter Twenty-three

Almost at once Cole's eyes picked out the shape of a single horse and rider. He had passed the guards at the edge of town, so the single shot must have meant that one of them had been too nervous with his gun and fired before realizing that this was neither Keldson nor one of his men.

There was something odd about the rider, odd about his shape in the saddle. Cole began to run again. He caught the horse's bridle in front of the hotel. Looking up, he recognized Dick Walters in the faint starlight.

The man's head sagged forward and lolled to right and left with the movements of his horse. One of his hands tightly grasped the saddle horn. The other hung limp at his side.

Reynolds and another man ran up the street toward him. "Get Doc Holt," Cole ordered. "Bring Doc to the hotel."

He eased Walters out of the saddle. Then, as he would carry a child, he lifted Walters into his arms and went toward the lobby of the hotel.

"Have to risk a light," Cole told Reynolds who had gone ahead to open the door. "But pull the blinds soon as you get it lit."

Reynolds struck a match, found a lamp and lighted it. While he moved around the lobby lowering the shades, Cole laid Walters on the leather-covered sofa. Blood had soaked Walters's left sleeve and dripped from the fingers of his left hand. Cole opened his pocket knife and gently cut the sleeve away.

What Cole saw made his face go a shade paler. The bullet had struck just above Walters's elbow, smashing the bone. Bits of it were imbedded in the torn flesh. Miraculously, the bullet and shattered bone had missed the main artery, and the only damage was to veins which bled slowly and steadily.

Walters was a ghastly shade of gray but he was conscious. He looked at Cole, whispering, "They caught us —"

"Don't talk," Cole said. "Save your strength."

"No. I've got to tell you. Maybe it'll help. They caught us at Rodinski's place. There was six of us then, but Keldson had his whole crew. Rodinski got killed. The others ran. I got it in the arm."

"What about the fires?"

"Keldson herded the families outside, then he fired their buildings. Haystacks, too. Rodinski's wife wanted to patch me up, but I knew you'd want to know."

The man who had gone after Holt came in, pushing the stumbling, drunken doctor before him. Just inside the door Holt stumbled and fell. He lay motionless on the floor, groaning, wheezing, and cursing under his breath.

Cole swore bitterly. "Go fetch Sidonie Carew," he said to the man who had brought the doctor. "Tell her to bring a whole pot of hot coffee. Tell her it's Doc."

The man left on the run. Reynolds said, "Let me handle him, Knapp. I'll get him up."

But Cole shook his head. "This is a job I don't want botched."

He walked down the hall back of the lobby, opening doors and searching for clean linens for bandages until he found them. Returning to the lobby, he looked around until he found a bottle of whisky behind the desk. He poured it straight over Walters's shattered arm. The man gasped and passed out.

Gently, moving the arm as little as possible, Cole wound the clean strips of cloth around it. "He'll have to wait till we can get Doc sober enough to work on him."

Cole sat down wearily in a chair and stared at Walters. How could a man live with an arm cut off? How could he operate his ranch?

He thought of that first time he had met Dick Walters when the man had tried to act the tough hand that he wasn't at all. Cole had been all wrong in his judgment. The ride Walters had just made showed what was in him. The same hard core of courage would be found in the others who had stayed, Cole thought. Reynolds. Al Sands. Tom Binn. Probably all of them.

Sidonie came in carrying a steaming graniteware pot of coffee. She went to work on Doc at once, wordless after Cole hoisted him to a sitting position, propping him against the back of the couch.

Patiently, gently, Sidonie labored with the doctor, talking, urging him to drink the scalding brew. He drank, though he protested loudly.

Cole watched her, watched the gentle expression in her eyes, watched the straight line of her back as she knelt on the floor. He was amazed at her understanding. She didn't condemn Doc for his weakness as most women would. She took people as they were.

He felt tenderness for her, and it was this expression she saw on his face as she glanced up at him.

Cole said, "Can you handle this? I ought to be outside. No telling when Keldson will show up."

"I'll get him on his feet," she said, her voice sure and calm. She glanced up and smiled. "Be careful." He nodded and went out.

Again he glanced eastward, looking for gray along the horizon. It had been a long night and it seemed to him it should be over, but he knew it wasn't. Halfway maybe. Still a long way to go.

Upstreet he suddenly heard the beat of a running horse's hoofs. Then it died and a man yelled, "Hey! Where's Knapp? I want to talk to him."

Cole turned to Reynolds who had followed him outside. "One of the Regulators?"

"Don't think so. Sounds like Larsen, one of Chain's men."

Cole ran up the street. Silence here, except for the sound of his boots on the hard ground. Sands and the other guard were waiting for the Chain rider to enter town before firing their signals. But the Chain man held back.

When Cole reached the last house, he called, "How many with you?"

"None. I'm alone."

"Then ride in with your hands in the air. If you're trying to run a sandy on us, you'll die in the saddle."

"Just want to talk to you," the man said.

He sounded scared, but he came on, hands raised in the air. He drew rein before Cole. Impatiently Cole asked, "Well, what is it?"

"Keldson sent me. Said to tell you he'll let the town alone if you ride out. It's you he wants."

"Not Miss Carew?"

"You, I said."

"If I don't?"

"He'll wipe the town out. Like he burned —"

"Better not talk about that," Cole said. "There's a dozen guns on you right now. The men behind those guns had friends on Big Horse."

"Well, you coming?"

Still Cole did not answer. He tried to weigh this in his mind knowing the odds that would be against him if he rode out of town. He would be a dead man once Keldson had him, but there was a chance he could get Keldson before he died. That, he knew, was the only way the town could be saved, and in the long run the only way Sidonie could be saved. If he died and Keldson lived, nothing could save Sidonie's life.

"You gonna stand there all night?" the Chain man demanded. "Or are you going with me?"

"I'll go," Cole said. "Reynolds, fetch my horse."

Silence for a long moment, then there was sound of movement. Cole shifted his glance from the Chain rider, but he didn't see his horse. Several townsmen crowded around him.

"You can't ride out there," Al Sands said gruffly. "Keldson will cut you down."

"Rather see the town burned?" Cole asked.

Sands hesitated, then he said reluctantly, "Well, hell yes, if it comes to that."

Cole said harshly, "Where's my horse?"

Again the silence, broken only by the shuffling of feet in the street dust. This time it was Reynolds who spoke. "We're not letting you go, Knapp. You're a damned fool for even thinking about it."

Then Tom Binn, "What about the rest of you? Knapp saved the town by blowing up Keldson's tunnel. Hell, it ain't even his fight. It's ours. You going to let him die to save our skins?"

There was a murmur of dissent that rose until individual voices were audible. "Stay here, Knapp." "We need you." "You can't trust Keldson. He'll rub you out and then come after us."

Cole turned to the Chain rider. "Looks like I'm staying. Now you take a message back to the Chain crew. I'm going to kill Keldson. When I do, the rest of you better fork your broncs and make trail out of here. Not one of you will be safe after tonight. Tell 'em that."

The man turned his horse without speaking and rode away. When he cleared the town, he broke into a hard gallop.

"You'll hold the town, boys," Cole said. "You'll hold it now."

More deeply moved than he could ever recall being before, he turned toward the hotel, calling back over his shoulder, "Two shots if you hear them coming, Sands. Don't worry about the Regulators. We'll have to get along without them."

As he walked along the street, Cole

thought that a man could find courage anywhere if he looked close enough. There was Walters for instance. And Frank Lynn, who had come to warn them. Now the townsmen who would not surrender Cole when they must have felt that surrendering him would save their lives.

When he reached the hotel, he found Doc sitting up. He held a cup in his trembling hand, drinking coffee as fast as he could. Occasionally he glanced at the unconscious Walters on the sofa.

When Cole came in, Sidonie said, "See if the water's hot in the kitchen. Doc's got to clean up before he can touch that wound."

Cole went on through the lobby to the kitchen. He tested the boiler of water on the big range. Scalding but not yet boiling. He picked up the boiler and carried it into the lobby, along with a bar of soap and a towel. The doctor was on his feet. His eyes were clear, and he was staring at Walters with professional interest for the first time.

"Hope I never catch you looking at me that way, Doc," Cole said.

Holt removed his coat and vest and rolled up his sleeves to the elbows. He said, delving into his black bag, "Get out of here, both of you. This won't be pretty. Maybe you'd better send Reynolds in. He's worked with me before."

Cole took Sidonie's reluctant arm and guided her out of the lobby and onto the porch.

Chapter Twenty-four

Cole sent Reynolds into the lobby, then he stood on the hotel veranda with Sidonie, staring out across the silent town. A glow caught his eyes across the creek where he judged Davis's wood yard would be. He watched it a moment, finally deciding it was only the reflection of something else.

Why hadn't Keldson struck? What was keeping him? Had he mastered his temper and gone back to Chain? Had he been sated by the destruction of the ranches in the upper valley?

No, those answers weren't good enough. But sly as he was, he might have returned to Chain to wait, hoping that the additional hours of waiting would break the townsmen's will to resist. Then another possibility occurred to Cole. Keldson might have run into trouble with his crew.

"What about Keldson's crew?" he asked Sidonie. "Are they the same men who worked for Chain when your dad was running things?"

"A few," Sidonie answered, "but most of them are men Marty hired after Dad began to fail. The old hands quit because they couldn't get along with Marty."

Down at the lower end of town another glow suddenly caught Cole's attention. This one required no squinting to see. It flared as a huge match might flare, and instantly a sheet of flame leaped across the wall of a building. The saddle shop, Cole thought, next to the church.

Coal oil! So Keldson had struck. He'd sent a man ahead of the crew to fire a building. Cole had known from the first what would happen if Keldson thought of this. The town's defense would crumble. The townsmen would forget Keldson momentarily. They would see nothing but the fire, the most deadly threat that a wooden frontier town could know.

Cole ran into the street. Already the flames had lighted up the lower end of Main. In the glare Cole saw the townsmen running toward it, their rifles gone, buckets and shovels in their hands.

"Let it burn, damn it," Cole bellowed. "Can't you see you're doing exactly what Keldson wants you to do?"

But they had no ears for him. He was reminded, looking at them, of horses he had once seen trapped in a burning stable. Their eyes were wild, filled with fire's nameless fear.

They jostled him as they passed. He leaped into the path of one of them and was nearly brained by a swinging shovel. Then he stood alone in the middle of the street.

He heard Sidonie scream; he felt the thunder of hoofs as a vibration in the ground beneath his feet. So Keldson had won. He'd burned the ranches and now he'd burn the town. Tomorrow would see the final exodus streaming down the valley toward the San Miguel, like refugees trying to escape the blight of war.

Cole's hand dropped to his gun butt. He swung around, the fire to his back, to face the east, the direction from which Keldson and his riders would come.

"Cole," Sidonie called. "Get out of the street."

He looked at her blankly, not moving. It seemed to him that there was no chance now, that Keldson won, and that Andy Carew had lost.

Sidonie left the hotel and ran toward him. Keldson's riders entered from the upper end of town. No shots. No one there to challenge them now. Sidonie threw herself at Cole. "Have you gone crazy, Cole, standing out there by yourself?"

He picked her up and carried her to the hotel veranda. "I guess I did, but I'm all right now. You stay here. No matter what happens, you keep under cover."

Then he was gone, disappearing into the shadows beside the hotel. As he ran, he heard a scream, but it was not Sidonie's scream. It was Walters's shriek of pain from the lobby of the hotel. Cole's body chilled with the sound of it but his anger only grew.

Another sound, one he could not identify, then it was drowned by the thunder of shod hoofs in the dusty street. They pulled up before the hotel, a dozen of them, Keldson's big, hulking shape among them.

Keldson's arrogant voice went out, "Find that damned drifter. I want him dead. A thousand dollars to the man that gets him."

They began to spread out to search the town. They'd go through the hotel. They'd find Sidonie. What then? Cole had to fight the impulse to step into the street and show himself for that wouldn't do Sidonie any good. There'd be a better time. There had to be. Ben Davis was around somewhere. And Frank Lynn over there in the Staghorn. One of them would cut loose. Or both.

Again Keldson's raging voice rose above the clatter in the street, "Two of you watch that bunch fighting the fire."

The odd and nameless sound that Cole had heard before was louder now. Apparently it caught the ears of the riders in the street. They halted as if puzzled, perhaps fearful.

Cole moved forward to the corner of the hotel, and paused there, the shadows still hiding him. The sound was louder now, like distant thunder, but more metallic than that. A rock slide from the rim of the mesa? Cole glanced upward, but could see nothing in the darkness. He looked eastward, and saw at last the line of gray that marked the coming dawn.

Inside the hotel Walters screamed again.

Keldson, evidently irritated by the delay, bellowed, "Move, damn it. They're getting the fire under control down there. It was only coal oil. The wood ain't had time to catch. And find that drifter."

Again the crew moved as though to disperse. Glancing downstreet, Cole saw some of the townsmen, their sanity regained, returning along the street but now armed only with shovels. Behind them the dying fire glowed and hissed as the men who remained behind threw buckets of water upon it.

It was darker in the street, the man-and-horse shapes more blurred and no longer clearly outlined by fire. Keldson shouted, "Larsen, start another fire."

"Where?"

"Anywhere. What the hell do I care?"

Larsen whirled his horse. Cole lifted his gun and shot the man out of his saddle. Instantly the whole group swung toward him. Hastily aimed bullets probed the darkness for him. The sky in the east grew brighter and laid a gray pall of half-light upon the town.

Frank Lynn opened up from the Staghorn, but was cut down almost at once. Cole suddenly felt all his planning had gone for nothing. The townsmen in the street with shovels. Ben Davis nowhere in sight. Sidonie inside the hotel. And all that Cole could do was to stand here alone and fight and probably die.

Keldson was lost among the milling horses. They had started toward Cole, but now they seemed disorganized. The noise Cole had heard became a thunderous racket. At last he could place it by its sound. He looked toward the bridge.

What he saw shocked him into immobility. It was the great steam tractor of Ben Davis, smoke pouring from its stack twenty feet into the air, flame belching beneath it.

He heard the clanking it made, like the sound of a thousand anvils beaten all at once. As he gaped at it, the steam whistle shrieked, so shrill and loud that it nearly burst his ear drums.

The tractor rolled on across the bridge and came toward Main, traveling on the slight downgrade at the speed of a galloping horse. It headed straight for Keldson's riders. Their horses reared and plunged. They tried to run, and balked by their riders' hands on the reins, began to buck and pitch.

The townsmen, running, cut to the side of the street, heading for the upper end of town where they had left their rifles. And still the tractor came thundering on. It left the side street and swung into Main. Its whistle shrieked again, rattling every pane of glass in town.

Cole couldn't keep from grinning. Davis was hidden behind the bulky steam boiler, probably crouched down between it and the mandrel of his wood saw. Cole could imagine the look on his face. There would be a wicked, almost boyish pleasure in the old man's eyes. And there would be something else: a fierce delight because at last he had a chance to even up for Keldson's murder of his son.

The Chain horses were rearing and plunging, bucking savagely to rid themselves of the stubborn men who still fought to hold them.

A Chain rider sailed through the air and hit one of the veranda posts with his head. He lay motionless. Another slid off the rump of his rearing mount and was pounded to death beneath the hoofs of the other horses.

Now the townsmen, led by Judge Benson, stalked downstreet toward the scene of confusion, rifles in their hands. The tractor stopped in mid-street. Its whistle sounded again.

Keldson was out in the open; his men had scattered. Of all the Chain crew, Keldson alone kept his head. Holding his rearing horse with one hand, he pulled his revolver with the other and fired regularly and methodically at the tractor. Cole threw a shot at him and missed, fired again and missed. Keldson, a poor target in the thin light, whipped around in the saddle of his bucking horse.

One of Keldson's bullets pierced the

boiler. Steam shot a full twenty feet toward him, momentarily enveloping him in a white cloud. Other bullets ricocheted off the tractor's steel to be lost in the willows along Big Horse Creek.

Two more Chain crewmen lost their fight to stay in the saddle and were thrown to the ground. One crawled to the safety of the hotel veranda, dragging a broken leg. The other got up and ran, to be stopped by the townsmen and their threatening rifles.

As suddenly as it had begun, the terrific hubbub of noise stopped as the last of the boiler's steam sighed out. The tractor sat there, lifeless, ordinary, in the street's deep dust, a dead and unfrightening thing in the dawn's gray light.

Keldson roared, "Dismount and fight. What do you think I'm paying you for?"

Cole stepped into the street. For an instant he was unseen by Keldson who was swinging from the back of his big roan on the side away from Cole.

Another horse was coming down the road from Chain. Cole risked a glance in that direction. It was Zelda.

Chain's riders were swinging down when Cole's voice snapped out like a whip, "Hold it. Stay in your saddles. Drop your guns."

He had no real hope they would comply,

but Davis had given the town the time it needed with his shrieking tractor. They were ready now.

The Chain men hesitated, looking toward Keldson. Cole said sharply, "Keldson! Come out from behind that horse."

Keldson's reply was a bullet, triggered from beneath the horse's neck. It tugged at the brim of Cole's hat, but the shot, right beneath the nose of the already panicky animal, made him rear with fright. For an instant Keldson stood exposed.

As Keldson fired, his men had whirled to face the townsmen, and the street became a bedlam of racketing rifle and shotgun blasts. Men cursed and fell, or fell quietly. Somewhere a man moaned steadily.

Cole, unconscious of the blasting guns around him, centered his gun on Keldson's chest. No thought of Andy now. No thought of anything. Only concentration on Keldson, momentarily visible behind the rearing horse. The gun bucked against his palm; he heard the roar of the shot; he saw the flash of fire.

Keldson's gun fired; smoke blossomed from its muzzle. The bullet smashed into Cole's shoulder and spun him half around.

Cole forced himself to turn back, his left side numb from the shoulder to waist. He brought his gun into line again.

But he didn't fire. The need was gone. Keldson swayed, fell, and lay still.

And now, the silence was broken only by Cole's harsh breathing, then by the running feet of Sidonie as she crossed the hotel veranda to come to him.

Zelda had yanked her horse to a halt, slid off, and now knelt beside her son.

Cole glimpsed her there as the world whirled and swam before his eyes. Then Sidonie was beside him, supporting him, and Ben Davis was on the other side. They were walking with him toward the bridge and the safety of the Davis house.

Cole's last look down the street told him there would be no more trouble with Chain. What was left of the crew was being herded toward the jail by a pompously strutting Dusty Rhodes and a humbled Judge Benson, the rest of the unhurt townsmen following. The last sound he heard was the bitter sobbing of Zelda as she crouched beside Marty Keldson's body.

Then he was across the bridge, passing the stream of women and children coming from the Benson house. Davis kept calling reassuringly, "It's all right, Mrs. Johnson. Your man's all right." Or, "Joe's hit, Nellie, but not bad. He had a cigar in his teeth when I left."

Janet met them at the door, her baby in her arms. "So it's over," she said. "I guess it will be a good world for little Bud after all."

"Sure it will," Cole said.

"I'll get the doc," Davis said, and wheeled and ran toward the bridge.

Janet went into her room and closed the door. Cole looked down at Sidonie. It seemed a long time since he had knelt beside Andy in the dust of the street of San Ramon, a long time measured by what had happened. But the job was done, and Andy would be pleased.

"I didn't intend to kiss you a while ago," he said. "I wanted to wait until it was finished."

"But you aren't sorry, are you?" Sidonie asked, smiling at him, the worry finally gone from her.

"No, I'm not sorry," he said, and putting his good arm around her, drew her to him.

The employees of Thorndike Press hope you have enjoyed this Large Print book. All our Large Print titles are designed for easy reading, and all our books are made to last. Other Thorndike Press Large Print books are available at your library, through selected bookstores, or directly from us.

For information about titles, please call:

(800) 223-1244
(800) 223-6121

To share your comments, please write:

Publisher
Thorndike Press
295 Kennedy Memorial Drive
Waterville, ME 04901